"The Bluford Series is mind-blowing!"
— *Adam A.*

"These books are *deep*. They show readers who are going through difficult problems that they are not alone in the world. And they even help teach you how to deal with situations in a positive way."
— *Vianny C.*

"I want to confess something: before I started reading the Bluford Series, I didn't like to read at all. Now I can't stop."
— *Mariela M.*

"Each Bluford book starts out with a bang. And then, when you turn the page, it gets even better!"
— *Alex M.*

"I love that these books are about the hardships young people face. They show we are resilient and can overcome anything."
— *Kennedy T.*

"These are life-changing stories that m___ you think long after you rea__ ___ ___ ___

"I found it very ___ these books. The__ beginning to end a___ The characters are __ ___ the endings left me in eager anticipation of the next book."

ADELANTE

"For the first time in high school, I read a book I liked. For real, the Bluford Series is *tight*."

— *Jermaine B.*

"These are thrilling, suspenseful books filled with real-life scenarios that make them too good to put down."

—*DeAndria B.*

"My school is just like Bluford High. The characters are just like people I know. These books are *real!*"

— *Jessica K.*

"I never liked reading until I found the Bluford Series. These books have descriptions that play like high-definition movies in my head. They are fantastic and should be read by everyone."

— *Yoriell P.*

"Each Bluford book gives you a story that could happen to anyone. The details make you feel like you are inside the books. The storylines are amazing and realistic. I loved them all."

—*Elpiclio B.*

"One of my friends told me how good the Bluford Series is. She was right. Once I started reading, I couldn't stop, not even to sleep!"

— *Bibi R.*

"I love the Bluford books and the stories they tell. They're so real and action-packed, I feel like I'm inside the pages, standing next to the characters!"

—*Michael D.*

Girls
Like Me

Tanya Savory

Series Editor: Paul Langan

TOWNSEND PRESS
www.townsendpress.com

Books in the Bluford Series

Copyright © 2016 by Townsend Press, Inc.
Printed in the United States of America

9 8 7 6 5 4 3 2 1

Cover illustration © 2015 by Gerald Purnell

Excerpts of Maya Angelou's "Caged Bird" from her poetry collection entitled *Shaker, Why Don't You Sing?* New York: Random House, 1983.

Townsend Press, Inc.
439 Kelley Drive
West Berlin, NJ 08091
permissions@townsendpress.com

ISBN: 978-1-59194-470-6

Library of Congress Control Number:
2015952203

Chapter 1

Angel McAllister held her phone away from her ear and winced.

"*Seriously?*" yelled Sharice Bell, Angel's best friend. Her piercing voice crackled through the tinny speaker. "You don't think Trey is into you? You know he's always looking at you in English class, right?"

"Just because some boy looks at me once in a while doesn't mean he's into me," Angel replied. "I'm pretty sure Trey doesn't look at me like *that.*"

"Girl, what planet do you live on?" Sharice scoffed. "That boy looks at you, like, every five minutes. He's obviously trying to get your attention."

"No, that's not it," Angel said as she closed her bedroom door and flopped on her bed. "He only looks at me when Mr.

Collins asks a question. All he's interested in is whether I'll answer it so he won't get called on."

Sharice sighed. "Well, you could at least look *back* at him and smile or something! You just stare straight ahead like you actually care about Collins and his stupid poetry."

"Well, I *do* like poetry. Some of it, anyway," Angel replied, hoping to change the subject. "Have you started that poetry assignment yet? I can't believe we're going to have to read our work in front of the whole class next week!"

"Whatever," Sharice grumbled. "Can we get back to the topic of Trey and your love life? Tomorrow when he starts staring at you, you better smile at him. I'm gonna be watching to make sure you do. If he smiles back, ask him if he wants to go to the eighth-grade graduation party with you."

"I don't know," Angel said, shifting uncomfortably on her bed.

"C'mon, Angel! You know Trey is *fine*, and I've never seen him with a girl. Whenever I ask Marcus why Trey isn't seeing anyone, he says it's 'cause Trey's real shy. So what you gotta do is—"

"Can we just drop it?" Angel cut in.

Marcus was Sharice's boyfriend, and ever since the two of them had gotten together, Sharice insisted Angel needed a boyfriend too. Marcus's twin brother, Trey, seemed like the obvious choice to Sharice. Nothing Angel said seemed to stop her from trying to hook them up.

"I'm not asking Trey Jones out to the party, so let's stop talking about it."

Sharice huffed dramatically. "You sound just like Marcus. Every time I ask him about getting Trey with you, he gets all mad and tells me to drop it. So, you don't even think about Trey? How can you not be interested in him at all?"

A familiar nervous twinge fluttered in Angel's stomach. She rolled over on her bed and stared up at the tea-colored stain on her ceiling. It had been there since she and her family had moved in three years ago. The first time she saw it, Angel thought the stain looked like a bird in flight. Sometimes, like now, it almost seemed sad, like a lonely creature trapped in her room.

"It's not that I don't want to. It's just . . ." Angel paused to find a response that would satisfy Sharice. "It's just that my mom says I can't see boys until high school."

3

"Your *mom?*" Sharice grumbled. "Why does she even need to know? Please, if my mom knew everything I did, I would never be allowed out."

"You're right about that," Angel laughed. "You'd be staying home with me."

"It's true! That's why you should just go. Find an excuse or whatever. Just don't tell her."

"I'm not doing that. She'd kill me if she found out," Angel lied.

Only weeks ago, Mom had asked her if there were any boys she liked at school.

"They're all so weird," Angel had said. It was a vague, meaningless answer that had stopped Mom's questions. Angel had used the tactic many times since moving from Virginia to California with her little sister and parents. Fake answers, Angel discovered, were easier than admitting the truth—that she had trouble making friends and felt out of place most days.

Sharice was Angel's closest friend in Lincoln Middle School, but lately Angel felt as if Sharice was changing, growing away from her somehow.

"But high school is practically here!" Sharice's voice crackled through the phone again, breaking her thoughts. "We've only got a few days of eighth grade

4

left. I mean, your mom is gonna let you go out with boys over the summer, right?"

Again Angel paused. Sharice didn't wait for a response.

"Oh girl, you gotta talk to her. Now! Tell her *everyone's* gonna be at the graduation party. It's not like you'll be alone with Trey or anything. Tell her that *all* the girls you know are already hanging with boys. Tell her you *have* to go to this party with a boy, okay?"

"Okay," Angel said without any enthusiasm. "I'll try. But don't get your hopes up."

"That is just sad," Sharice said with a dramatic sigh. "We're gonna have to talk more about all this. I gotta go now, though. I just got a text from Marcus and I gotta see what's up with him before Mom gets home and starts bugging about me being on my phone too much. Later, girl," Sharice said and hung up.

Angel sat up on her bed and flipped through the stack of fashion magazines Sharice had made her borrow last month. "*You really should look at these,*" she had said when she left them. Angel stopped on an article in an old edition of *Youth Swag* called "Perfect Teen Style." It was full of pictures of girls her age and a few years older.

They all look so happy, like they don't have a worry in the world, Angel thought as she stared at the broad smiles, flawless hair, and curvy shapes. In one picture, several girls were laughing as if they had just heard the funniest joke on earth. A beautiful dark-skinned girl with bright lipstick and huge earrings gripped her stomach as if the laughter almost hurt.

Angel couldn't remember the last time she had laughed that hard. Maybe a year ago? She and Sharice had gone to the movies, and Sharice had drunk a large soda so quickly it made her burp loudly right when the movie was totally quiet. People in front of them turned around, and Angel began to giggle. Then Sharice accidentally belched again, and both girls burst into such loud laughter that they had to run out to the lobby. It took them nearly ten minutes to calm down and tiptoe back to their seats.

That was before Sharice changed. Now all she ever talked about was clothes, boys, and parties. Whenever Angel suggested doing some of the things they used to do, like riding bikes to East Park or making up recipes for pizzas (once they created a truly horrible pickle

6

and pineapple one), Sharice would roll her eyes. Since the start of eighth grade, she frowned upon anything that didn't seem "grown up." Riding bikes was for children. Giggling at burps was out of the question. Instead, Sharice had started forcing style and fashion magazines on Angel and making blunt comments about her looks.

"Girl, you have got *to do something about that hair. In case you didn't know, it's sticking straight out in back like a shelf or something,"* Sharice had said this morning when they rushed by each other in the hallway after first period.

Angel closed the magazine and reached back self-consciously to feel her hair. Was it still messy? She got up and stared at herself in the mirror next to her dresser. A thin girl with cinnamon skin and large brown eyes rimmed by oversized glasses peered back at her. Angel tilted her head and eyed herself critically. She thought her nose was too flat, her shoulders too narrow. Her legs too lanky, and her arms too skinny. Angel pushed her hair behind one ear so that she could see the small gold earrings her father had given her the last time he visited. He had told her that she was getting prettier every single day, but Angel doubted it. She forced a weak smile at her reflection and then shook her head.

"I'll never be like those girls in the magazines," she said quietly. "I'm not like them. Not at all."

Angel sat back down on her bed and pushed the magazine aside. She reached under her mattress and pulled out a tattered notebook with the words "English Class" written on the front. It was a disguise Angel had invented so no one would ever open it. In reality, the notebook was her journal, the one place where she confessed her deepest thoughts, dreams, fears, and hopes. She glanced down at her first entry from the week they arrived in California:

Our first dinner here: hamburgers, which is something Mom usually knows how to cook. But these ones tasted like old cardboard. Yuck! I hope dinners here won't always taste this bad.

As dull as the early entries were, writing them had made Angel feel better after the move. Her journal gradually became like a trusted friend, a place where she could talk about anything and everything. Each time she wrote, she felt a rush of excitement, as if she were sharing a secret. Lately, her secrets had grown more complicated.

Angel opened to a new page and jotted down the date: June 13. She glanced up at the trapped bird on the ceiling and began to write.

I'll admit it. There IS someone in our class that I would love to go to the party with, but can you imagine? THAT could never happen. Could it? Sharice would freak out. So would everyone else, I'm pretty sure. What would happen if I asked

"Angel?"

There was a tap on Angel's door and Dionne, her seven-year-old sister, opened it. She was holding onto Ellie, her old stuffed elephant, and sniffling a little. She frowned at Angel and stood in the doorway looking gloomy.

"What is it, Di?" Angel said, giving her a smile. Her little sister was Angel's favorite person, even when she was grumpy.

9

"I'm hungry, and there's nothing happening in the kitchen *at all*," Dionne moaned. "I asked Mom, but she told me to leave her alone."

Angel looked at the clock by her bed. *6:45*.

Not again, she thought to herself. Angel tucked her notebook under her pillow and walked over to Dionne.

"Well, let's go make something happen in the kitchen," she said, putting her arm around her sister's small shoulders. "How about if we make some pancakes in the shape of hearts?"

"Mmm, breakfast for dinner!" Dionne cheered. Her frown instantly turned into a broad grin that revealed a missing front tooth. Dionne had waited for the Tooth Fairy for two days when it fell out at the babysitter's last week. Mom kept forgetting, so Angel finally snuck into Dionne's room and hid a dollar under her pillow.

"*I* knew *she'd come!*" Dionne had cheered the next day. It was great to see her sister's excitement, but it wasn't enough to erase Angel's growing worries about Mom.

Angel sent Dionne into the kitchen to grab some bowls. As they passed the living room, Angel saw her mother sitting on the sofa in a haze of cigarette smoke. It was the fourth time this week that Mom spent the evening chain-smoking in front of the TV.

"Are you hungry, Mom?" Angel asked carefully. The first time she found Mom like this and asked her, Mom had blown up and yelled at her to leave her alone.

"No. There's leftovers in the fridge, I think," Mom answered, her face worn and expressionless, her eyes glazed.

Angel sat down next to her, unsure what to do. Up until a couple of weeks ago, Mom had always been strict about keeping the apartment neat. She had insisted on sitting down to a home-cooked dinner at 6:30 on weeknights. She used to yell if Angel left a dirty sock on the floor or wandered in late. Now, dishes were piled in the kitchen, and ashes covered the dusty table in front of the television. The only leftovers in the refrigerator were a jug of week-old milk and some dry, shriveled pizza from one of the nights Mom hadn't felt like getting up off the couch.

"Are you . . . sick?" Angel asked gently. "I can get you an aspirin or something?"

Mom fanned the air and coughed. "No.

Just low on energy. I think I'll be better in the morning." She stared blankly at the TV, where a celebrity chef yelled at a contestant who had undercooked some chicken.

Angel sighed. She doubted Mom was going to be better any time soon. When Dad had first left them four months earlier, Mom was like this for a few days, but then she snapped out of it. She went to her job at Essentials Salon as always. She wore her bright dresses and fixed her hair perfectly. Except for a day or two, dinner was always on the table at the same time.

Then, two weeks ago, Mom ran into Dad and his new girlfriend at the grocery store near their apartment. Angel had been there with Dionne flipping through magazines while Mom had run off to the produce section. That's when Angel heard her father's unmistakable nervous laugh. Dionne heard it too.

"*Is that Daddy?*" she had asked, dropping a sticker book and looking up at Angel with wide eyes.

Angel knew Dionne struggled with the idea of her parents splitting up. It took her three months before she stopped asking if Dad was going to come back home from his trip.

"I think so," Angel had said.

Dionne had raced down the aisle toward the sound of Dad's voice. When she and Angel reached him, Dad was holding a bag of chips and a jar of salsa. He looked as if he had just swallowed something rotten. Standing next to him was a beautiful young woman with smooth brown skin who reminded Angel of the perfect girls in Sharice's magazines.

Dionne stopped and gawked at the woman, who had her hand on Dad's back.

"Nice to meet you," Mom had said, her voice strained and hollow sounding. Mom's eyes had focused more on the floor than at the pretty young woman.

"And . . . and these are my girls," Dad said with another burst of nervous laughter. *"Angel, Dionne, this is my . . . my . . . friend, Anita."*

Angel mumbled a vague hello. She didn't like seeing this strange new woman touching her father in such a familiar way. She hated thinking about what was really going on. Dionne huddled close to her, as if it were raining and Angel was an umbrella.

"Well, we're, ah, running late for a party, so . . ." Dad had said as he

13

scratched his head and looked away. *"Nice seeing y'all."*

Anita smiled and waved goodbye by waggling all the fingers on her right hand. Then she winked at Angel as though she knew a secret. It made Angel feel kind of sick.

"Good Lord," Mom said when Dad and Anita disappeared. She grinned an odd tight-lipped smile and went back to picking out apples, her movements shaky and rough. Later that evening, Mom had laughed a little too loudly at dinner when Dionne asked if the pretty woman with Daddy was a movie star.

"Not in any movie I want to see," Mom had said.

Later that night, Angel thought she heard her mother crying. The next day, Mom overslept and didn't seem to care that her skirt was wrinkled or that her mascara was smudged. Then the long evenings of smoking and staring at the TV started. Angel even found empty wine bottles on the counter a few times. Before that Saturday, she had never known her mother to drink. Now she wondered when it would stop.

Angel took a deep breath and gently brushed ashes off her mother's lap.

14

Mom pushed her hand away.

"Stop fussing over me, Angel. I'm fine!" she huffed. "Go help your sister."

I'm trying, Mom, Angel thought to herself as she left her mother and hurried into the kitchen to cook dinner.

I'm trying.

Chapter 2

"So did your mom say yes?" Sharice asked the next morning.

Angel had waited at the corner of Greene Street as Sharice rushed to catch up with her on the way to school.

"Say yes to what?" Angel asked blankly. She had left her mother sitting at the table just moments earlier. Mom had barely spoken, though she did sigh and rub her temples as if she had a bad headache. Angel made sure Dionne had lunch money and that she knew her babysitter, Mrs. Alexander, would get her after school.

"To *what?*" Sharice squeaked. She wore a snug denim skirt and a bright pink top that showed a bit of her stomach when she walked. Angel felt dull and lifeless next to her in her worn jeans and a wrinkled black shirt. "Are you serious?"

"Yeah, what?"

"To you going with Trey to the party!" Sharice yelled. "It's only a week away. Come on—twin brothers! The two cutest boys in the school! It would be the best ever. Think of how jealous everyone would be. Please don't tell me you forgot to ask your mom."

Angel shrugged. She wished Sharice would forget it. Couldn't they talk about something other than clothes and boys?

"I guess I got too busy," Angel said. "I had a ton of homework last night. Our poems for Collins, remember?"

"Girl, that's what you always say," Sharice sighed. "Ain't no one got so much homework that they can't take a second to say, 'Hey Mom, can I go to a party? Everyone else is going.'"

"Well, my mom wasn't feeling well last night, so I didn't want to bother her."

"Excuses, excuses," Sharice said and poked Angel playfully with a tube of lipstick she pulled out of her purse. "I can see you're gonna need some help. I gotta figure out how I'm gonna get you two together. Now let's see . . ."

Angel tuned her out as they walked. It

was a warm late-spring morning with high fluffy clouds and the faint smell of the ocean in the air. Lincoln Middle School stood back from the street like the shy younger brother of Lincoln High. The two buildings were next door to each other, separated by an enormous parking lot and athletic fields. Lincoln Middle was a yellowy two-story stucco building shaped like a big L, while the high school was an imposing brick structure with sprawling wings and branches that dominated the block. To Angel, it seemed that whenever they walked by the school, there were groups of loud teenagers leaving or arriving, some in their own cars.

When Angel started sixth grade, the high school kids always seemed so grown-up. She and Sharice had walked by them quietly then, sneaking peeks at what they did and how they dressed, catching some of them smoking or kissing outside. No one ever noticed either of them back then. But now, as Sharice walked by in her tight skirt, a few boys stared at her and made comments.

"What are y'all doin' going over there?" a tall boy in a football jersey called out. "You two don't look like you belong in middle school!"

Sharice grinned and looked right back at the group of boys as a security guard watched.

"Y'all better get ready for me, 'cause I'll be up in Lincoln in a minute," Sharice said with a wave, clearly flirting. Angel noticed Sharice swung her hips a bit, and she spoke with confidence. Angel didn't know how she did it. With high school just a few months away, she felt awkward whenever the older kids said anything to her. Just last week, a Lincoln boy with a faint mustache had asked Angel if she had change for a dollar. She had gotten so flustered that she spilled her entire backpack on the sidewalk.

"Girl, I don't need your books," the boy had joked when her English book tumbled toward his feet.

Two older girls sitting on the steps had snickered. Angel glanced at them and felt like a sixth-grader again—not the graduating eighth-grader about to join them.

"Why didn't you say anything to him?" Sharice said in a low voice, jabbing Angel back to the present. "That boy was talkin' to both of us!"

Angel glanced back at the boy in the

jersey and quickly looked away when she saw that he was grinning at her.

"I don't even know him," she said with a shrug.

Sharice rolled her eyes. "Angel, don't you know *anything?* That's how you *get* to know a boy. What am I gonna do with you?"

Angel wished Sharice would stop giving her advice about boys. She was relieved when they finally reached the middle school's wide front doors.

"One thing's for sure," Sharice continued, eyeing Angel up and down. "You gotta stop dressing like you're cleaning the house or something. And a pair of beat-up Converse? Girl, you're a serious fashion emergency."

"Yeah, I ran out of clean things to wear," Angel said as they entered the crowded hallway. She thought of the mountain of dirty laundry piled on the floor of their apartment. Normally, her mother would do a load every few days, but not lately. The old Mom would never let Angel leave the house wearing something so wrinkled. The new Mom didn't even notice. Angel did, but she forgot when Dionne asked her for help finding an outfit for school.

"Look, I gotta go, girl," Sharice said, scanning the bustling corridors. "I want to catch Marcus before the bell rings. See you in English, and—" Sharice grabbed Angel's hand, a playful glint in her eye. "Don't forget! I'm gonna be thinking up that plan to get you and Trey together, so be ready. And maybe put some lipstick on before class. And check your hair. And don't forget—"

"Sharice!" Angel snapped.

"Bye," Sharice said with a grin. She turned and headed quickly down the hallway. "Gonna get you a boyfriend," she added in a singsong voice as she disappeared in the direction of Marcus's locker.

Angel tried to forget the conversation as she headed toward her first period class. On the way, she passed the school library and spotted her reflection in the glass doors. There again was the familiar brown-eyed girl with the thin face and chunky glasses. Only this time, those eyes were stormy. Self-consciously, Angel reached to smooth her hair and straighten the wrinkles in her shirt.

"It's pointless," she grumbled, annoyed at what she saw. And yet Angel knew her clothes and hair were not the real reason she suddenly felt so irritated. There was something else bothering her too: Sharice.

I don't want her to get me and Trey together, Angel thought as she pushed through the crowd. *I don't want Sharice to get me together with any boy.*

Math and history classes were normally interesting, but today Angel felt as if she were trapped in a heavy fog. All through class, she kept picturing Mom's blank expression at breakfast. Had she even gone to work?

What about dinner? Laundry? The dishes? Do I have to do it all? Angel wondered. *And for how long?* She had asked the same questions in her journal late last night, though it wasn't all she had written. For a second, she imagined her mother at home on the couch reading it page by page. The thought made her shudder.

"So, Angel, give us one example."

Angel jumped, accidentally knocking her textbook off her desk. It hit the floor with a loud slap. Ms. Warner, her history teacher, eyed her from the front of the room.

"I . . . I . . . what?" Angel stammered, feeling completely lost.

Giggles erupted in the classroom. Angel reached down for her book. Nearby LaDonna Burns, a popular girl who Angel had once seen dump chocolate milk on a frightened sixth-grader, smirked and shook her head. Angel made it a point to avoid LaDonna as much as possible, though Sharice had started hanging out with her this year.

"An event," Ms. Warner said crisply. "Tell us one event that helped spark the Civil Rights Movement."

Angel's mind went blank. She had read the chapter on Civil Rights, but with all the distraction last night and the entire classroom staring at her, she couldn't remember anything. She flipped open her book, hoping the pages might trigger a memory.

Ms. Warner sighed. Angel's face began to burn with embarrassment.

Ask someone else, Ms. Warner, she pleaded wordlessly. The teacher kept waiting.

Suddenly Angel saw a hand to her left go up like a lifeline. Win Liu, an Asian-American boy who transferred into her class last year, had raised his hand.

Win was in two of Angel's classes. He was always friendly but was unpopular in school because he was different and he was a good student. Sometimes boys would tease him, calling him a teacher's pet or even making fun of his name. Once Angel saw him get tripped by guys in the hallway.

"What about that kid who got killed for whistling at a white woman?" Win asked.

The room suddenly grew silent. Angel felt the stares of her classmates shift from her to Win. She was grateful to be free of the attention.

"Boy, what textbook are you readin'?" LaDonna asked with a snort. "Ain't nothin' in here about someone being killed for *whistling*."

"But it happened, LaDonna," Ms. Warner said somberly. "Win's right. Emmett Till was only a year or two older than you. He was murdered for whistling and flirting with a white woman in 1955."

"That's messed up," said one student. Others shook their heads. The class was silent for several long seconds.

"I don't remember hearing about that," a tall girl named Justice Waters said quietly.

Angel glanced over at Justice. She was the opposite of Sharice in many ways. She rarely wore makeup, and she didn't seem to care too much about fashion. Today she wore a baggy black T-shirt with the words *East Park Steppers* written in large white letters across her chest. And yet Angel still thought Justice looked pretty with her light hazel eyes, high cheekbones, and long beaded braids. Some girls made fun of Justice's looks and lack of style, but she never seemed to care. Sometimes Angel found herself staring at her.

"What page was it on?" Justice added, flipping through her history book. "I woulda remembered *that*."

"Oh, it's not in our book, but it should be," Ms. Warner said. "How did you learn about it, Win?"

"My grandmother told me," he explained. "She saw my homework last night, and we started talking about it."

"Are you serious? Your granny checks your homework! She tuck you in at bedtime too?" LaDonna snorted from the back row. A few students laughed until Ms. Warner shot them a warning glare. Win nervously ran his hand through his hair and looked embarrassed.

Angel wanted to reach out to him somehow. She had always liked Win.

Once she even told Sharice that she thought he was funny. Sharice had wrinkled her nose in disgust. *"Yuck. They shoulda named him Lose instead of Win,"* she had said.

"But how could that happen?" someone else asked, snapping Angel's thoughts. "There ain't ever been a law against flirting with anyone."

"There was no *written* law," Ms. Warner explained, "but many people back then believed that it was wrong for black and white people to flirt with one another, let alone be romantically involved. They called it *miscegenation.* And it *was* against the law for blacks and whites to marry in much of the United States. Some people thought it was unnatural. Others said it went against the Bible. Still others were simply afraid of change."

"That's just wrong," Justice said with a toss of her braids. "My mom is white and my dad is black. I wouldn't even be here if those laws hadn't changed. How could people believe that?"

"Well, that's exactly the kind of question many people were asking in 1955," Ms. Warner said. "The death of Emmett Till got even more people questioning the laws and the unfair treatment of black people."

"So what really happened to Emmett?" LaDonna asked, leaning forward with a curious gleam in her eye.

Ms. Warner looked at Win and nodded to encourage him to speak again.

"They . . . um," Win began as he looked hesitantly around the room, particularly at LaDonna. "They beat him up real bad and then . . . threw him in a river, and he drowned."

Someone cursed in the back of the class. An angry silence spread through the room.

"Just for flirting with a white woman?" Justice said quietly, shaking her head. "Haters gonna hate. I'm glad I live today and not then. At least things have changed. Some things, anyway."

After class, Angel rushed to catch up to Win. "Thanks for bailing me out in there. I was totally zoning."

"Yeah, I saw you looking out the window," Win said shyly. "Then I saw Ms. Warner watching, and I knew she was gonna call on you. Glad I was ready."

"Me too," Angel said as they walked

down the hall together. "That's really cool that your grandmother remembers Civil Rights and everything."

"I know, right? She always surprises me with what she knows," Win said, shaking his head. He glanced at Angel, then at his watch, and back at her again. "So . . . it's almost the end of the year. Can you believe it?" he added suddenly, in kind of a nervous rush.

"I know," Angel said, wondering why he had changed the subject. "Seems like we just started and now . . ."

"And now it's coming to an end and . . . graduation . . . you know, I . . . I was wondering if . . . if," Win stammered. He paused and looked around as if he was searching for something. "Well, what I mean is, I wanted to ask you if—"

"Angel!" a familiar voice shouted from down the hall. "Come here! I gotta tell you somethin'."

Angel turned to see Sharice push between her and Win. Marcus was right behind her chewing on a straw. He looked at Angel and held up his hands as if to say, *This isn't my fault. I had nothing to do with it.*

"Wait a second, Sharice," Angel said.

She turned back to Win, but he was already backing away into the crowded corridor.

"Bye, Angel," Win said weakly, disappearing into the crowd. "I'll talk to you later."

Before Angel could say anything, Sharice began dragging her by the arm toward English class. "Don't say I didn't warn you," she said with a giggle.

"She just couldn't leave it alone," added Marcus as he headed in the opposite direction shaking his head.

"What are you talking about, Sharice?"

"So, here's what I did," she said in an eager, excited voice. "I just texted Trey and said that you liked him and that you wondered if he wanted to go to the party with you and—"

"You *what?!*"

Angel felt her stomach lurch. She expected Sharice to nag her to talk to Trey after class, but nothing like this. She was about to protest again when they rounded the corner and burst into the classroom.

Trey was at his desk. And he was staring straight at Angel.

Chapter 3

Angel froze.

What am I supposed to say? she thought desperately. If she admitted Sharice had made everything up, Trey might be angry at Sharice, and she would get mad at Angel. But if she went along with the lie, Angel realized things could get even worse. She suddenly felt trapped.

"Girl, don't just stand there blocking the door," Sharice said, giving Angel a gentle shove to nudge her forward. "Just see what he says."

Angel wanted to crawl under her desk and disappear. She darted quickly to her chair and sat down. A hot wave of embarrassment spread over her as she opened her English book and flipped to the poem Mr. Collins had assigned,

Maya Angelou's "Caged Bird." The words were like a temporary refuge.

The free bird leaps
on the back of the wind
and floats downstream
till the current ends
and dips his wings
in the orange sun rays
and dares to claim the sky.

"Angel?" A low voice interrupted her reading.

She turned to see Trey leaning toward her from across the aisle. He had a puzzled expression that looked to Angel like a cross between fear and embarrassment. She opened her mouth to speak, but no words came out. Trey scanned the room as students steadily filed in. Angel wondered if he wanted to hide that he was talking to her.

"Sharice texted me earlier," he began in a nervous voice just above a whisper. "And, well, you know, it's just that . . . I'm kinda seeing someone else . . ."

Two seats away, Sharice, who had been leaning out of her chair to listen, nearly toppled over. She caught herself with a thud on the desk in front of her. A few students turned at the sound.

"What are you talkin' about?" Sharice squeaked. "You got a girlfriend? I've never seen you with *anyone*. Marcus never said anything about that. Seriously?"

Trey rubbed his forehead and shook his head. "No . . . I mean, yes. Maybe. I guess."

"What're you tryin' to say?" Sharice demanded. "You mean you're taking some other girl to the party?"

Trey looked from Angel to Sharice and then back at Angel. A few drops of sweat beaded on his forehead. More students turned at their desks to listen. Angel wished she could escape from the classroom. Somehow Trey looked the same way. Finally, after several agonizing seconds, he blurted out, "No . . . I mean . . . what I meant to say was . . . I'm going with Angel."

"All right!" Sharice cheered with a wide grin. "My brother will drive us, and we can all go to Grillz before the party for burgers. This is gonna be *on point!*"

Trey turned around and nodded weakly at Sharice. While his back was turned, Angel glared at Sharice and shook her head angrily. Sharice ignored her and started pulling books from her bag, humming happily.

Just then, Mr. Collins strode into the classroom and began taking attendance. Unusually tall and broad, Mr. Collins looked more like a linebacker than an English teacher. He had a full bushy beard, a booming voice, and he often seemed uncomfortably constricted in the dress shirts and ties he wore. Occasionally he would loosen his tie so it hung slack around his neck. As big and gruff as he was, Mr. Collins often became emotional when discussing his favorite poems. Sharice and other students thought he was strange, but Mr. Collins was Angel's favorite teacher. Yet today, she didn't want to see him— or anyone.

Mr. Collins opened his book and started pacing in front of the class. He read silently for a moment and then stared toward the back of the room, his gaze faraway and tender, as if he were looking at a beautiful sunrise instead of a cinderblock wall.

Angel heard a few stifled snorts of laughter from students behind her. Then Mr. Collins boomed out a stanza of the poem he had assigned for homework:

"The caged bird sings
with fearful trill
of the things unknown
but longed for still
and his tune is heard
on the distant hill
for the caged bird
sings of freedom."

Mr. Collins finished reading and sighed, his eyes suddenly misty.

"So, what is Maya Angelou saying?" he asked, moving between rows of students. "Earlier we saw a free bird floating on the breeze and claiming the entire sky as his own. Here Angelou presents a caged bird with clipped wings. And yet the caged bird sings. Why?"

Silence filled the classroom. A few students shifted in their seats. Someone nearby coughed. Angel knew her classmates expected her to answer. It's what usually happened, but now her thoughts were clouded by what Sharice had just done.

Why didn't she listen? Why does she think I need a boyfriend? The questions came to Angel in waves, but one stuck in her mind with a voice louder than the others.

Why do I feel so different from everyone else?

Angel looked around the classroom, her eyes suddenly burning. It seemed as if all the girls she knew had changed in the past year. Like Sharice, they chattered nonstop about boys, parties, and the clothes they wanted to wear to parties to impress the boys. More and more often, Angel felt as if she was on the outside looking in, watching everyone else move along happily and effortlessly while she felt trapped.

"Anyone?" Mr. Collins asked. He caught Angel's eyes just as she wiped them. "Angel? What do you think?"

Please, Mr. Collins. Not now, she wanted to say.

Instead she took a deep breath and stared at the poem. She felt like that bird, shut in a cage watching the free birds having the time of their lives.

"Well," Angel said finally, looking up from her book into Mr. Collins's eyes. "I don't know why a trapped bird would ever sing. I would think it would want to cry, instead."

"I just wish you hadn't done that," Angel said to Sharice as they walked home after school.

It was a warm Friday afternoon, and Angel squinted at the sun that glared down at them. The older apartment buildings and squat stucco homes that lined her street looked small and uncomfortably close as she walked. The few weedy yards near her house seemed imprisoned behind their chainlink fences. Angel thought they almost looked like small jails.

"But it worked!" Sharice replied. "You're going to the party with the cutest boy in our class. And I can say that, because Marcus is his twin," she added with a grin.

"Don't you get it?" Angel asked, her voice rising, anger bubbling in her chest. "I don't want you fixin' me up with someone I hardly know. And I can tell Trey doesn't even want to go with me. He only said yes because he was embarrassed and wanted you to stop asking him in front of everyone!"

"Don't worry—it's all good," Sharice said in a hurry. "You're finally goin' out with a boy, Angel, and it's about time. I had to do it. I mean, you haven't even kissed one yet, have you?"

Angel winced. *Not again*, she thought.

The last thing she wanted to do or talk about was kissing boys. The thought made her feel awkward and uncomfortable.

"I kissed a boy last summer when I was visiting my grandma," Angel lied quickly. "It wasn't a big deal."

Sharice stopped walking. "You *what*? You never told me! What was his name? Was he older? Was he cute?"

Angel shook her head quickly, realizing her mistake. "It was just a quick kiss at a party at my cousin's," she said. "I don't remember his name or anything."

"That ain't a real kiss," Sharice huffed. "It doesn't count if you can't remember."

Angel felt as if she had just been slapped. Sharice must have noticed, because she immediately put her hand on Angel's shoulder.

"Look, Angel, don't worry. I'm gonna do your makeup and help you pick out an outfit at the mall tomorrow and everything. You're gonna look incredible," she said with a smile.

Sharice's words seemed silly to Angel. She had seen her own reflection in her bedroom mirror this morning. Plain. Confused. Drab. Those words fit. But not *incredible*. And yet she could feel boys beginning to notice her, especially lately.

And then there was Win.

He was getting ready to ask me to the party before Sharice butted in, Angel remembered.

Of all the boys in her class, Win was the one boy Angel thought she would actually enjoy going to the party with, but only as a friend. She wondered if he would be okay with that.

"You know, I think I'd rather go with Win," Angel confessed. "He was about to ask me when you and Marcus walked over."

"Win?!" Sharice recoiled as if she had just smelled something rotten. Then she burst out laughing. "Girl, now I *know* you've lost your mind. You'd have to be crazy to want to go to the party with that boy when you could go with Trey."

Angel shrugged. Why did Sharice care so much about who she went with?

"Seriously, Angel. Get real," Sharice finally said. "Win is Chinese. You're black. Plus he has a strange haircut and wears weird clothes."

"What difference does any of that make?" Angel asked angrily. "I like Win. He's smart and funny, and he's always nice."

"Whatever," Sharice sighed.

The two walked in silence for a moment before Angel felt Sharice's hand rest on her shoulder. "Look, I'm sorry if I was pushy about hooking you and Trey up. But you *gotta* go with him. I promise we're gonna have a blast. And once Trey sees you all dressed up, he's gonna wish he got with you a long time ago. You'll see. Plus, *everyone's* gonna be jealous of us going with Trey and Marcus. It'll be awesome!"

Just then Angel heard the rumble of a bass beat. A blue sports car full of teenagers slowly passed by. The music throbbed louder as the rear window opened. LaDonna Burns leaned her head out of the car.

"Hey, Shar!" she shouted. "See you tomorrow morning, girl!"

Shar? Angel wondered. No one ever called Sharice that.

"You know it!" Sharice waved back with a grin. She then turned quickly to Angel as if she owed her an explanation. "LaDonna's gonna meet us tomorrow at the mall. Her cousin's the manager of Style One!"

"What?" Angel asked. "You're kidding, right?"

"Nope. LaDonna says her cousin

knows all the best deals and when new stuff's comin'—"

"No, I mean about LaDonna meeting us. She doesn't want to hang with me. Does she even know I'm gonna be there?"

"It's only gonna be for a little while. This way we can all go to Style One together," Sharice replied, gazing at the disappearing car with an almost dreamy look. "LaDonna's cool with it. She's cool with everything."

Angel sighed. Sharice's excitement at being friends with LaDonna made her uneasy.

"Well, I'll check with my mom and see," Angel said as they made their way back to her apartment building. "I don't know how long she's going to let me stay at the mall. And I doubt she's gonna give me money for an outfit for a party she doesn't even know I'm going to!" *And that I don't even want to go to,* Angel thought to herself.

"It's all good," Sharice repeated with a broad smile as she turned up her block. "Everything's gonna turn out perfect. You'll see."

In her room later that night, after getting Dionne to bed and trying unsuccessfully to talk to Mom, Angel grabbed the secret notebook she had hidden in her mattress. She took a deep breath and reread what she had written yesterday evening:

I'll admit it. There IS someone in our class that I would love to go to the party with, but can you imagine? THAT could never happen. Could it? Sharice would freak out. So would everyone else, I'm pretty sure. What would happen if I asked

Angel felt her heart pounding in her chest. She glanced around the room, making sure her door was shut and that she was completely alone. The pen suddenly felt powerful in her fingers. She inhaled deeply and moved it to where she had left off.

She felt her fingers tense up and the pen begin to slide, the slick ink forming words before her eyes, words she had never said and could barely admit, though she'd felt them for some time.

What would happen if I asked . . . Justice to go with me?
What if I like girls more than boys?

Chapter 4

"Ten dollars?" Sharice huffed and rolled her eyes. "How are you supposed to buy anything with *that?*" She and Angel weaved through the crowded mall Saturday afternoon to meet LaDonna at the food court.

"My mom doesn't get paid until next week," Angel lied. The truth was she didn't ask her mother for a cent. The ten-dollar bill was leftover money from her birthday. She decided not to mention the graduation party to Mom after listening to her talk with Aunt Gwen on the phone early this morning.

"Charles and that girl are going to be living together barely a block away!" Mom had fumed from behind her closed bedroom door. *"I swear, Gwen, I don't know what I'm gonna do. It's like the*

world's crashing in, and ain't a thing I can do about it."

When Mom finally came out of her room, Angel pretended she didn't notice Mom's eyes were swollen and bloodshot and that she looked as if she hadn't slept in days. Just thinking about it made Angel shudder.

"There she is!" Sharice hooted. She tugged Angel over to a table where LaDonna was sitting in snug jeans and a tight T-shirt that hugged her curvy body. She stared at her phone, stabbing at the screen with a quick claw-like finger, and popping gum loudly. Her hair was almost perfectly straight, like a sleek black curtain draped along her face and resting with a healthy sheen on her chest. Angel could tell LaDonna had extensions. From Mom's work at the salon, she knew it took a lot of time and money to get her hair to look that way. And yet LaDonna acted as if she never worked hard for anything. She seemed bored as they approached, barely looking at Angel, though she did give Sharice a weak smile.

"Girl, you are lookin' *good*," Sharice said with an approving nod. "I don't know how you do it!"

"My cousin hooks me up," LaDonna explained, popping her gum with a proud smack. "And it's always good stuff, nothing tired or trashy." LaDonna eyed Angel's clothes as she spoke. Already Angel wanted to leave.

The girls ordered French fries and sodas and grabbed a larger table where they could watch everyone walking by. Right away, LaDonna spotted a few boys she knew from Lincoln High and waved wildly at them. Angel sipped her drink while Sharice and LaDonna chattered about people they knew, rumors they heard, and clothes they wanted. It seemed as if Sharice had forgotten Angel was even there.

At one point, an older boy in skinny black jeans walked by. He had tinted horn-rimmed glasses and close-cropped hair bleached to an almost gold color, and he wore a T-shirt with words on the front. *Free Spirit.*

"Oh my God. Look!" LaDonna leaned toward Sharice and lowered her voice. "It's Jeremy, the boy I told you about who graduated Lincoln High last year. He's totally gay. He's the one everybody called Super Fag."

Angel cringed at the ugly words.

"Is he for real?" Sharice asked as she dipped some fries in a red pool of ketchup. "He's like something you'd see on TV."

As they watched, Jeremy met up with a tall skinny white kid with blond hair and a large Adam's apple. The two boys hugged briefly.

"Tell me I'm not seein' this," LaDonna added with an exaggerated expression as if she was about to get sick. "Yuck."

Angel watched in silence as the two guys exited the food court together. She fidgeted with the napkin container in front of her, remembering what she had written the night before.

"Eww! You see that, Angel?" Sharice asked, giggling. "I can't believe it—in public, too!"

"Whatever," Angel said, still staring down at the napkin container. "It's not like they're hurting anyone."

Sharice gave Angel a funny look and then shrugged. "Yeah, but it's still weird. I've got a cousin like that. When my uncle found out about him back in the day, he kicked him out of the house."

Angel looked up, shocked. *"What?*

45

That's terrible! I mean, how could a parent do that to their own child?"

"He didn't want him around his younger brother. I wouldn't want someone like that around my little brother either. Would you? They hurt kids and stuff," Sharice said, scanning the crowded food court. "Anyway, who cares? I'm glad it's not our problem."

"But that's not true," Angel blurted, shaking her head, her pulse beginning to pound. "I mean, gay people don't hurt anyone. They're usually the ones that get hurt—"

"Why do you sound so upset all of a sudden?" LaDonna cut in, a curious expression on her face.

"Nothing. It's just—"

"How come you aren't seeing any boys?" LaDonna added, not waiting for an answer. Her eyes glimmered as if she had spotted something valuable. "Maybe you're like Jeremy . . ."

A stinging heat rose to Angel's face. Her cheeks burned with anger. She wanted to say something, anything, but the words were caught in her throat.

"No, you got it all wrong!" Sharice said quickly, coming to Angel's rescue. "Angel's just shy, that's all. Trust me, I know," she assured LaDonna. "Plus, she spends totally too much time studying. That's why she's makin' A's while I'm makin' C's!"

Angel smiled weakly at her friend, but her heart felt as if it were slamming against her ribcage.

"Anyway, Angel's going to the party next Friday with *Trey*," Sharice added, practically singing his name as she nudged Angel with her elbow. "And you know that boy is fine. Almost as fine as his brother."

"*What?*" LaDonna asked. Her voice rose suddenly. "Trey? How'd that ever happen?"

"Trey's been checking out my girl all year," Sharice explained. "He finally made his move this week!"

Angel cringed at how fake Sharice's description was. LaDonna seemed bothered by it, too.

"That don't make sense," she said icily. "I've known Trey since third grade, and I ain't never seen him checking anyone out, especially not Angel."

Sharice cleared her throat and glanced nervously at LaDonna, then back at Angel. The food court suddenly felt awkward and tense. *Get me outta here!*

Angel thought to herself.

"Well, I mean, it's not like it's solid yet or anything," Sharice began. "What I mean is that I *think* Trey might . . . But maybe not. It's hard to tell."

LaDonna grunted and sipped her drink. Then she grabbed her phone and glared at it as if she were trying to burn a hole through it with her eyes.

Suddenly, Angel realized why LaDonna was so angry.

Trey. She had a crush on Trey.

That's why she's hanging out with Sharice, Angel thought as she stared at her soggy fries. *She wants Sharice to hook the two of them up. Now I'm in the middle. No wonder she hates me.*

Angel wished Sharice had known about LaDonna's crush before the non-sense with Trey started. Now it was too late.

Angel could feel LaDonna's anger radiating across the table like heat from a fire. Angel glanced at her watch and tried to think of an excuse to leave. She had no desire to go to Style One. This whole thing with Trey was ridiculous. But even worse, the way Sharice had talked about gay people made Angel feel uncomfortable and alone.

What if she knew what I wrote last night? Angel wondered.

For years, she had heard people use the word *gay* as an insult or to describe something stupid. But some of these same people were nice otherwise. They had no idea their words were cruel, no idea she had been wrestling with these questions for months. Years maybe. They had always been there, like last night. Like right now.

The mall seemed to fade as a terrible thought occurred to Angel.

What would happen if Mom knew?

Angel had heard her mother refer to gay people as "messed up" now and then. She knew Mom believed it was unnatural for two people of the same sex to be together. Recently, they had watched a news story about gay marriage and Mom had grumbled, *"That is just so wrong. That's not what marriage is. I never thought I'd see something like this become legal."*

What would Mom do if she found out? Angel wondered. *Maybe she'd throw me out like Sharice's uncle.* And then another idea hit her like a hammer. *What if Mom never allowed me to see Dionne again?* Angel felt as if a sinkhole had opened

49

beneath her, threatening to swallow up everything and everyone she loved. Losing Dionne would be a pain she could not endure, a loss from which she could never recover. Angel shuddered.

"Hellooo? Earth to Angel!" Sharice's voice snapped her out of her thoughts.

"You comin' with us, or you just wanna sit here and stare into space?" LaDonna growled. She pulled Sharice ahead as they headed over to Style One, both of them in a deep discussion about hoop earrings.

Dazed, Angel followed along and found herself in a dimly lit store pounding with dance music. All the women in the store dressed like the ones in Sharice's magazines. Angel felt strange and out of place.

"Here you go, Angel. You gotta get this. It'll look so good on you," Sharice said, pointing to a slinky, one-shouldered, iridescent teal top. "LaDonna's cousin can sell it to you at half price."

Even with the discount, Angel didn't have enough money. She tried to explain, but Sharice wouldn't listen.

"Just get it. You can pay me back later," she insisted, giving Angel a twenty-dollar bill. Angel could barely hide her embarrassment, particularly with LaDonna listening to every word.

"I don't think my mom would even let me wear this," Angel said quietly, wishing she had never come to the mall.

"You do everything your momma says?" LaDonna asked.

"Just do what I always do, Angel," Sharice said, ignoring LaDonna's question. "Put it on after you leave your house, and your mom will never even know. It's easy!"

Angel sighed. Sharice had the same stubborn glimmer in her eyes that she had in school when she set her up with Trey. Angel was about to turn and walk out, but before she could, Sharice grabbed the top and turned to LaDonna's cousin.

"She'll take it," she announced.

"Sharice!"

"Trust me, okay. We'll go right home. I'ma put a full outfit together for you. You're gonna look *so* good! After you see what I'm gonna do, you'll be glad you got it. And if not, you can return it. Okay?"

"But, I don't even—"

"*Trust* me," Sharice repeated with a determined grin. "I got this, girl."

Angel bit her tongue. She liked the

idea of spending the rest of the afternoon with her old friend, away from LaDonna and her angry eyes and mean comments.

Reluctantly, she agreed. An hour later, they were back at Angel's apartment.

"Wait till you see what this looks like," Sharice said holding the skimpy top while Angel unlocked the door. "Girl, you are gonna look fly."

Inside, Angel spotted Dionne sitting alone on the couch in front of the TV. The volume was turned high, and Angel noticed she had arranged all her stuffed animals next to her on the couch, as if she wanted company.

"Where's Mom?" Angel asked, grabbing the remote and turning the volume down.

"Taking a nap," Dionne answered. Her hand was in a bowl of dried cereal on her lap. It was something she sometimes ate for a snack, but Angel immediately wondered if she'd had any lunch.

"Did you eat?"

"Not since breakfast. Mom said I can have cereal," she added.

Angel sighed. "C'mon, let's make you lunch." Angel looked down the hall toward Mom's room. The door was closed.

"Your Mom okay?" Sharice asked.

"Yeah, she's just been a little sick this week. Flu or something," Angel explained. "She's getting better now. Just tired."

Dionne watched Angel, but she didn't say anything. Angel could tell her sister knew she was hiding the truth. "You mind if I make Dionne a sandwich? It'll just be a minute."

"That's fine," Sharice said, picking up the bag with the top and fishing it out. "You still got your magazines? The one from April has something I think we can do for the party."

"Yeah, they're in my room on my chair," Angel said as she pulled out some bread and cheese. Sharice disappeared down the hallway.

"You think maybe we can do something fun tomorrow?" Dionne asked as Angel heated up a frying pan on the stove to make grilled cheese.

"Like what?"

"Maybe go to East Park like we used to. We can go on the swings. I can do the monkey bars by myself now. I'm faster than all the boys in my class, except Jordan," she confessed, clutching her toy elephant. "We haven't had fun in, like, forever."

53

"You're right," Angel said, recalling how they used to visit the park with Dad. It had been about a year since they had gone there. "Let's do it. You can race me. I might be faster than Jordan, though."

"Yay!" Dionne cheered. Her gap-toothed smile helped Angel almost forget LaDonna and the stupid shopping trip.

Angel grilled the sandwich until the bread was crispy and the cheese gooey, Dionne's favorite. Then she put it on a plate, cut it into triangles, and handed it to Dionne, who grabbed it eagerly.

That's when she remembered Sharice. Where was she?

"Sharice?" Angel asked.

There was no reply. Angel walked down the hall into her room to find Sharice sitting on her bed, a stack of magazines resting against her leg, her mouth open as if she were gasping for air.

A notebook rested in her hands. The words "English Class" were on the front cover.

Chapter 5

"What are you doing?!" Angel yelled.

The journal was opened to the most recent entry. Angel could see the question she had written the other night. She could see Justice's name, too.

"Oh my God, Angel," Sharice said, her voice rising with alarm. "What is *this*?"

Angel felt her knees weaken and her hands tremble. For a moment, she couldn't speak.

"You shouldn't be readin' that!" Angel's voice cracked as she snatched the journal away. "That's private! You're not supposed to be snooping in my room."

"I wasn't snooping. I was getting your magazines when I saw what I thought was your English notebook." Sharice pointed to the cover. "I thought I'd see if you'd started that poetry assignment."

Angel felt as if the room were spinning. Her notebook disguise had backfired! If she hadn't been distracted by Dionne, she would never have let Sharice in her room alone. Angel wanted to curse out loud.

"This can't be for real," Sharice said after a long, awkward silence. "I mean, this is just you tryin' to be funny, right?"

Angel didn't say anything. Sharice's eyes widened.

"No! You don't feel like that about girls, Angel. I've known you for years. You're not like *that*." Sharice spoke as if she were trying to convince herself. "Right?"

For a second, Angel thought she heard a note of concern in Sharice's voice. Maybe Sharice would understand—or at least try to understand. After all, they were best friends. They had shared all sorts of secrets since sixth grade. Maybe what Sharice had said at the mall was just her trying to impress LaDonna.

"It's really hard to explain," Angel began slowly. She leaned on the edge of her desk and took a deep breath. Sharice stared at her with a strange expression that Angel couldn't read. "It's not like I dislike boys, and I do think some of them are cute. But I don't feel about them like you do. When I think

56

about girls—"

Sharice sprang up from the bed. "I'm not hearing this," she said, shaking her head. She looked as if she had just taken a bite of something disgusting and wanted to spit it out. "The way you feel is *weird*. You ain't right."

The words hit Angel like punches. She tried to stand, but her legs felt weak, and her heart pounded like a hammer in her chest. "Sharice! Don't say that."

"You are *messed up*, Angel McAllister. I mean, that's *nasty*. And I can't *believe* you've felt like this all along and we've . . . we've been best friends!"

"We still are!" Angel pleaded.

"No we're not," Sharice huffed. "What will everyone think? They're gonna think I'm just like you—"

"You can't tell them!" Angel insisted. "It's nobody's business."

"Just keep away from me." Sharice recoiled from Angel as if she had a disease that could spread. "I'm *not* like you! I don't want anyone thinkin' I am. And I definitely don't want to be your . . . your *girlfriend*." Sharice spoke the last word with an exaggerated shudder of disgust.

57

"No, it's not like that!" Angel exclaimed. "I never meant that about you. I don't feel that way about you."

"But you feel that way about *Justice!* Who's next? Now I get why you're always asking me to come over and spend time with you alone and . . . oh, it's *so* gross!"

Angel felt as if her whole world were suddenly breaking apart. It seemed as if some massive wave had slammed everything and was now sweeping the pieces out to sea.

"Sharice, please! Don't."

Sharice turned and rushed down the hallway. Without another word, she yanked the front door open, stormed out, then slammed it shut. The thud thundered through the suddenly quiet apartment.

"What was that all about?" Mom yelled sleepily from her room.

"Nothing!" Angel shouted, slamming her own door shut and flopping on her bed, trying to comprehend what just happened. Tears in her eyes, Angel grabbed her journal and wrote what hurt most.

She's gone. My best friend is gone. She hates me . . .

*   *   *

Sometime later, Angel heard a strange, muffled sound coming from down the hall. At first, she thought it was Mom talking on the phone to Aunt Gwen again. But then it sounded like two different voices—upset voices. Angel slipped out of bed and tiptoed into the hallway to listen.

"Oh, this is just horrible!" she could hear her mother saying in a disgusted voice. "I can't believe this."

What was Mom talking about? And was that Dionne crying?

The light was on in her mother's room, but the door was closed. Angel crept closer. She could hear her mother speaking in a hushed voice. Then she could make out the sound of Dionne sniffling and asking "Why?" over and over again.

Angel tapped on the door. Both voices stopped.

"Mom? What's wrong?"

A hushed silence answered. Angel opened the door and found her mother sitting on the edge of the bed, her eyes unnaturally swollen and bloodshot from crying. She wrapped her arms protectively around Dionne, as if Angel were a threat to them both. Dionne reached out to Angel, but Mom slapped her hand down and shook her head.

"Don't you touch her!" Mom scolded.

"What is it?" Angel whispered in confusion. "What's going on?"

Mom pulled something out from under the covers of her bed—Angel's journal! She held it up in the air and shook it so hard that dozens of pages fell out and fluttered to the floor.

"No!" Angel gasped. "Wait . . . let me explain. I wanted to tell you, but—"

"There's nothing to explain!" Mom hissed. "I don't want to hear your excuses. And don't you dare come near your sister ever again. You hear me?!"

Again Dionne reached out to Angel, but Mom yanked her back.

"You made your choice. Because of your decision, you're not welcome in this house anymore," Mom's voice seemed to change and become distorted as she spoke. "Get out. Get out right now!"

"But Mom . . ." Angel begged as her room began to spin. Everything was suddenly hazy and blurred. A roar like rushing water filled her ears.

"Out! Out! OUT!" Mom repeated, her voice even louder and more forceful.

Angel felt herself beginning to panic. She reached to her ears to block out the noise, but the sound grew louder.

"OUT! OUT! OUT!"

She screamed.

Angel sprang upright and found herself sitting on her bed, sunlight streaming through her window. Outside a car alarm blared over and over again. She could hear Dionne down the hall giggling about something. Next to her, the notebook slipped and fell to the floor.

Only a nightmare, Angel thought weakly, leaning back in relief.

Angel picked up her notebook and looked at the last few lines she had written:

> *What am I going to do? I can't go to school. I don't even want to get out of bed. My world is over. Done.*

Angel hid in her room all day Sunday, pretending she was sick. When Dionne banged on her door for the third time to ask about going to the park, Angel snapped.

"Stop bothering me! I'll tell you when I'm feeling better."

"But you said we'd go to the park today—"

"I don't care what I said. I don't feel good. Leave me alone," she grumbled.

"Nobody wants to do anything around here," Dionne grumbled. "You're just like Mom."

A stab of guilt joined the misery already pooling in Angel's chest. She knew why Dionne wanted to go to East Park. Part of her wanted to go there too. It was a place they had gone when things were easier and happier. Before Dad left and Mom became a broken spirit. Before her classmates went boy crazy. Before she wrote the words in her notebook that changed everything.

The last time they had gone to East Park was just before the school year. Dad bought them ice cream, and they sat on their bench. Dad called the spot his corner because from there he could see everything: the swings where the girls played, the picnic tables where families had cookouts or played chess, and the small quad where street performers sometimes gathered.

Angel could still remember what he said to her. *"You're almost in high school. You must be pretty excited."*

"Excited? More like scared!"

"Scared?" Dad had said, raising his eyebrows. "Why?"

"I guess I worry that I might not fit in. I mean, I don't care about being really popular or anything, but I want to have friends," she had explained.

"Of course you're gonna have friends, Angel. What makes you think you won't?"

She shrugged. The gnawing questions lurked in her mind then, though she didn't dare mention them.

Dad had put his arm around her shoulder when she didn't answer. "Tell me what you think the most fun thing to do in high school would be."

"The most fun?"

"Yeah. Something totally different from middle school. Something new."

Angel had almost been embarrassed to admit her answer.

"I always thought it would be fun to try out for cheerleading. You know, be part of a team."

Dad nodded thoughtfully. "Then you need to go for it."

"No way," Angel had said. "Girls like me don't get to be cheerleaders."

"Girls like you?" Dad repeated. "What does that mean?"

"I'm different, Dad. Not pretty enough. Plus, I'm kinda clumsy," Angel had admitted. She knew he wouldn't understand what she really meant. She was glad.

"Now you listen," Dad had said, leaning toward her intently. *"You've got to live your life. You only get one shot at this, Angel. If that is what you want, you've gotta go for it. Otherwise you're gonna sit back and regret that you didn't, and you won't have anyone to blame but yourself."*

Angel remembered Dad's words after he and Mom split up a few months later. *Had he been talking about himself that day?* Angel wondered. That visit to East Park was the last time they had really talked.

"How *could* you?"

Mom's wailing voice suddenly boomed through the apartment.

Angel peeked out of her bedroom door and saw her mother's back as she stormed toward the kitchen, her phone pressed against her cheek. Dionne stepped into the hallway from her room.

"You and that girl could have lived anywhere in this city, Charles! And you gotta go and move a block away? How *could* you?!"

Angel heard a plate shatter, followed by the sound of breaking glass. Dionne ran to Angel, her eyes wide with fear.

"You betrayed me. You betrayed your children. And now you're gonna rub it in our faces?! How can you do this? How can you sleep at night?" Mom screamed.

Angel covered Dionne's ears as two more crashes rang from the kitchen followed by Mom cursing loudly. Then, like a storm blowing over, everything stopped, except for the sad, muffled sound of Mom sobbing.

Angel crept down the hall to the kitchen. Her mother stood hunched and alone, an island in a sea of shattered glass. Tears rolled silently down her face.

"Mom?" Dionne asked, holding Angel's hand.

"Go back to your rooms, girls."

"Are you okay?" Angel asked, reaching out to her.

"Please, just go back to your room."

Chapter 6

Angel forced herself to school Monday morning, fighting dread with each step she took. When Sharice didn't meet her on their corner, Angel tried to convince herself things would be okay.

Sharice wouldn't tell anyone, Angel reassured herself. *We're best friends. She's not like that.*

But the second Angel walked into history class, two girls huddled at LaDonna's desk looked up and snickered. One of them, who usually sat near Angel, had moved to a different seat. The other whispered something to LaDonna and shook her head as if she smelled something foul. Then a boy sitting near the back began making kissing noises, and all of them started laughing.

Win turned and raised his eyebrows.

Angel sank in her seat.

"Hey Angel," LaDonna asked in a syrupy sweet voice, "how's your love life?"

Another burst of laughter erupted from the girls, but it died down the instant Ms. Warner walked in.

LaDonna knows, Angel thought, panic sweeping over her. *Sharice told her.*

"What's going on?" Win whispered as Ms. Warner turned her back to write an assignment on the board. Angel could barely bring herself to look over at him. Surely he must've heard. But then she saw the concern in his eyes.

"She's being a jerk, like always," Angel mumbled, nodding toward LaDonna.

In that quick glance, Angel caught something out of the corner of her eye that made her grip her desk. With Ms. Warner's back turned, LaDonna had pulled her phone out and was furiously tapping out a text. As soon as she finished, LaDonna waved at Justice and pointed to her phone. Justice sat with her arms folded and rolled her eyes, refusing to listen.

LaDonna leaned over and showed what she had written to one of her friends. Both girls began giggling.

"Anyone care to let me in on the

joke?" Ms. Warner asked coolly as she opened her textbook.

Angel stared straight ahead, her forehead beginning to sweat. She could still hear LaDonna's muffled snickering even after the other girl was quiet.

"LaDonna?" Ms. Warner said sharply. "Please tell the rest of us what's so funny."

"Nothin'," LaDonna finally said. "I just, um, heard a joke in the hall or somethin'."

Ms. Warner glanced up from her textbook. "Well, unless you want that joke to get you an afterschool detention, I suggest you keep it to yourself during class. And put that cell phone away. Understand? The rules haven't changed just because the year's almost over."

LaDonna sucked her teeth and smirked before slipping the phone into her bag.

"Man, Warner got eyes in the back of her head!" someone whispered.

Angel held her breath. She could almost picture LaDonna's text. It was bad enough that Sharice had betrayed her and LaDonna had told all her friends. Now Justice would find out that Angel had a crush on her. It almost made her sick to her stomach.

Just then, Angel noticed Justice glance at her and then roll her eyes toward LaDonna.

Maybe Justice won't believe it, Angel hoped. *Maybe everyone'll think it's another one of LaDonna's mean jokes, and in a day or two they'll forget it.* She stole a quick look around the room, and no one was looking at her anymore. Ms. Warner was talking quickly and holding up a book that had pictures of Civil Rights marches in Alabama. LaDonna looked as bored as usual.

Maybe it's all over, Angel thought. *Maybe that's it.*

Angel rushed out of history class, hoping to avoid LaDonna and Justice. She hurried, head down, toward English class, but Win ran up behind her and put his hand on her shoulder.

"You okay?" he asked. "What was going on in—"

"Dude, don't waste your time. She don't want you. Ain't you heard?"

Angel looked up to see Trevor and Omar, two eighth-graders from the boys' basketball team, blocking her path. Both were friends with LaDonna. Trevor, a muscular boy with a wolfish face, looked her up and down. He was smacking and chewing his gum just like LaDonna. Omar, a taller and skinnier boy with pointy elbows, nudged Win aside and put his arm around Angel.

"Nah, she just ain't met the right man," Omar said. "Spend time with me, and you'll change like *that.*" He snapped his fingers right in front of Angel's face, making her jump.

Angel tried backing away but bumped into the row of lockers behind her.

"Or just keep on with the girls and let me in on some of *that,*" Trevor added with a leer.

"Leave me alone!" Angel said, her heart pounding. She had never felt so scared in school. She tried ducking her head under Omar's arm, but he moved, blocking her path.

"Why you gotta be like that?" he asked. "Let me change your mind, girl."

"She said to leave her alone," Win warned. "Take your hands off her!"

Trevor turned around in surprise. Win glared up at Omar, who towered over him by nearly a foot.

"Win, don't!"

"You must be kiddin', Fortune Cookie!" Omar said with a loud laugh. "You need to leave before you get hurt. You hear me?"

Omar stepped forward threateningly, but Win didn't budge. Angel had never seen him so serious. Usually when kids picked on Win, he made a joke or just shrugged it off. This time he didn't flinch.

"Leave her alone," Win repeated. Angel saw his hands shaking. "And quit calling me Fortune Cookie. That's not even Chinese."

The two boys laughed, but Omar let go of Angel. She moved quickly to Win's side.

"C'mon, Win. Let's go. Forget this," she urged.

Students began gathering in the hall. Angel knew some were eager to see a fight. It was always that way.

"Oh my God. Is that *Win?*" someone asked.

"Yeah, and he's about to *lose*," a girl joked.

"That boy's fortune says he's gonna get a beat-down," another added.

Omar stepped closer to Win.

"You really wanna get hurt protecting your gay girlfriend?" he growled. "*You* ain't gonna make her switch sides."

Win opened his mouth to speak and

then looked at Angel with a puzzled expression.

"What?"

Omar and Trevor stared at each other. Their eyes bulged as the news hit them.

"He don't even know!" Trevor roared, his voice breaking into loud cackling laughter.

Omar doubled over as if he had never heard anything so funny.

"Don't know what?" someone asked from the crowd rapidly filling the hallway.

Trevor fought to catch his breath and pointed at Angel. "This boy don't know that he's tryin' to hook up with a *lesbo!*"

The word hit like a bomb blast. The hallway erupted in chatter as the news spread through the crowd like fire.

Angel felt as if she was about to throw up. Everyone in the hall turned to stare at her. Nausea churned her stomach. Faces became twisted and distorted, as though she was watching everything from underwater. Voices became muted and jumbled. Angel reeled backward a few steps, grasping for Win's arm to keep her from falling.

Suddenly a familiar voice thundered in the hall, cutting through the chaos.

"What exactly is going on here?"

boomed Mr. Collins. "Everyone, get to your classes!"

Students scattered. Trevor and Omar were gone in seconds. Soon only Win remained with Angel. Overhead, the bell for the next class rang. Angel felt the heat and confusion begin to lift, and she took a deep breath.

"What just happened?" Mr. Collins asked.

"Nothing," Win answered, hoisting his backpack up and avoiding the teacher's stern stare.

"It looked and sounded like a fight, Mr. Liu," Mr. Collins said. He turned to Angel and looked at her carefully. "Are you okay, Angel? Did someone hurt you?"

Angel shook her head, unsure of what to say or where to begin. She glanced at Win, but he avoided her eyes.

"I've gotta get to class," Win mumbled, turning his back on both of them. "Everything's okay, Mr. C. No problems." He hurried around the corner of the hall.

Mr. Collins sighed and yanked at his tie until it came almost completely undone. He looked at Angel again and raised a bushy eyebrow.

"You look as though you've just seen a ghost. But if you're sure everything's

73

okay, perhaps we should head to English class? I believe we're both—"

The bell blared overhead. Mr. Collins paused until it silenced. "Late," he added with a smile.

Angel caught her breath, taking in what he just said.

English class! In all of the confusion, she had not considered how awful it would be to face Sharice for the first time since she had read her journal. And then there was Trey! Surely he knew everything by now, too.

What if they're talking to everyone in our class right now? Angel wondered. *What if everyone is laughing? What if—*

"Angel?" Mr. Collins's voice was heavy with concern. "Are you sure you're okay? What's going on?"

Angel suddenly felt cornered. She needed to escape somehow—away from Mr. Collins's probing questions and the countless cruel whispers she knew awaited her in class.

"I think . . ." Angel began in a shaky voice. "I think I'd better go home. I'm not feeling well. I'll just go to the nurse's office and have them call my mom."

"Are you sure? I can walk you there if you need help," Mr. Collins offered, glancing at his watch.

Angel shook her head forcefully. "No. I'm okay. It's only down the hall."

Just let me go, Angel thought to herself, feeling her need grow more urgent. *Please. I gotta get outta here. Now.*

Mr. Collins studied Angel's face. He tugged at his beard thoughtfully. "Okay," he said finally, handing her a hall pass. "Feel better, Angel. Hope we'll see you tomorrow."

Angel nodded and tried to smile, but her heart was already racing. She was about to do something she had never considered.

As Mr. Collins disappeared into his classroom, Angel walked right past the nurse's office. Now that classes had started, the halls were mostly deserted. Keeping an eye out for other teachers or students, Angel headed down the quietest corridor in the school.

Finally, she reached the cafeteria entrance. She peered in the tiny wired windows of the steel doors. As she expected, the cafeteria was empty. Lunch wouldn't begin for another half hour. Angel knew if she tried to slip out the front doors of the school, someone would see her. But she remembered from a dance last year that the doors in the back of the cafeteria opened to the school parking lot. If she could reach them, she could sneak outside.

The thought pulled her like a magnet.

Without a sound, Angel slipped inside the cafeteria. She could hear the clanging of pans and the chatter of workers coming from the kitchen. Her heart pounded as she dashed to the rear doors. Somewhere nearby a radio was blaring, muffling any sound she made. Angel breathed in the aroma of soap and bleach and warming cafeteria food. Her fingers tingling, she grabbed the handle of the heavy steel door that led to the loading area.

Angel knew she should stop. Turn around. Go back to class. But she kept hearing Omar's laughter. Seeing La-Donna's mean eyes. Sharice's betrayal. All that and worse awaited her inside the school. She couldn't face it. Not now. She had to run.

Gathering all of her courage, Angel pushed against the door. With a quick shove, it opened to the middle school parking lot. Fueled by a rush of fear and relief, Angel flew outside.

Chapter 7

"Hey girl, you need a ride?"

Angel kept her head down, trying to ignore the older boys in the car that trailed her. She was only two blocks from school when they started following her.

"Where ya goin', girl?"

One boy leaned from the passenger-side window and beckoned Angel to come closer. Cigarette smoke drifted from the window and music pumped through the speakers in the car.

Normally, it would be easy to dismiss the boys. Sharice did it effortlessly with a joke or smile, often with Angel next to her. But those days were over. Angel felt vulnerable and alone on the street.

Just leave me alone, she thought bitterly as the car continued to shadow her. She wished she could just fly away where no one could see or bother her. Instead she walked faster.

"Why you in such a hurry?" the boy said. "We only wanna talk."

Angel was grateful to reach a one-way street where the car couldn't follow. She turned quickly. The boy hanging out the window yelled something rude, and the car moved on. Angel sighed and crossed another block before reaching a corner with a bus stop.

An old woman on a bench at the stop eyed her as she approached. The woman's hands were filthy. She clutched tattered shopping bags stuffed with what looked like blankets. Angel could feel the woman examining her.

"Ain't you supposed to be in school?" she said as Angel neared. "Your momma know you out here?"

It's none of your business, Angel wanted to say.

"She's got her own problems," she mumbled instead. The sad truth of her words stung as she said them.

The woman grunted and then began coughing loudly.

I can't talk to Mom, Angel thought as she walked past the strange woman. Her eyes suddenly burned, and her vision grew blurry. *I can't talk to anyone.*

She thought of the English class she was missing and imagined students talking about what just happened in the hallway. The rumors were probably spreading like wildfire. Angel could picture Trey cringing at the news as Mr. Collins droned on about the caged bird.

His wings are clipped and his feet are tied . . .

The line from the poem echoed through her head as she meandered along another city block. Far off, church bells rang mournfully. It was 11:00.

What am I gonna do for four hours? Angel wondered. She couldn't go home because Mom might be there and would find out she had cut school. She couldn't call Dad without everything exploding in her house. She didn't have money to go somewhere and get lunch. There were no friends to call, no places to hide. Strangers rushing by seemed to scan her as if they knew the secret Angel was hiding.

Then a thought hit her. There was one place she had escaped to in the past.

Could it help her now?

Angel felt her pace quicken. She weaved through familiar blocks almost unconsciously, her mind focusing on the destination like a sanctuary. Soon, Angel could hear telltale sounds in the distance. Children laughing. The metallic squeak of swing sets. Then she spotted the metal fence and the sign:

Welcome to East Park.

Angel rushed into the park, relieved to find something familiar and safe. Inside, preschoolers ran around as if they didn't have a care in the world. Angel could barely remember how that felt.

"You're lucky," she whispered at them, a wave of jealousy sweeping over her.

Nearby stood the old man with his dented hot dog cart and blue coolers full of ice cream sandwiches and popsicles. The June day felt almost as warm as when she had visited the park with Dionne and Dad last summer. The old man had been there that day, too. He even seemed to recognize her, giving her a gentle wave.

"Hey there! All alone today?" he asked.

Angel nodded and waved weakly as a young woman with a stroller approached him and ordered something for her child.

"Yeah, all alone," Angel mumbled,

remembering how Dad had joked with the old man about the Oakland Raiders. She didn't want to have to explain to him that Dad had abandoned them. That her parents had broken up. That she had just cut school.

Angel spotted where she and Dad sat during their visits to the park. With a lump in her throat, she collapsed on their bench and gazed at the noisy kids on the swings, the tired mothers checking their cell phones, the old man handing out napkins to a little girl.

Suddenly Angel missed Dad more than ever and wanted to sit beside him again. But then a train of thoughts crept into her mind.

What would Dad say if he found out about me?

What if he read my journal too?

Would he still love me?

Angel wrapped her arms around herself and leaned against the bench, a wave of weariness overtaking her. She wished she could be magically transported back in time to when everything was easy and uncomplicated. Back when they lived in Virginia and had breakfast as a family on Sundays, and Mom and Dad would tease each other while Dionne giggled in her high chair. It was all so long ago . . .

"All right, GO!"

"Left, left, kick, turnaround, kick!"

Angel bolted upright and looked around. She was still on her bench in the park but the light was different. The sun had shifted in the sky, and shadows now stretched across where she was sitting. Not far away, the old man was packing up his hot dog cart. Most of the strollers were gone. Angel rubbed her neck, stiff from sleep, and was startled by the sounds of rhythmic clapping, stomping, and chanting coming from nearby.

"East Park Steppers mix it up like . . ."

Angel stretched and glanced toward the sound to see a tall girl she recognized from Lincoln High leading a group of dancers in the middle of the quad. They stomped and clapped their hands in time.

"East Park Steppers gonna fly like . . . Hey!"

Angel had seen step teams before, but never in the park. Some of the steppers slapped sticks together as they stomped. Together they projected power and skill. As Angel watched, a few more kids wandered up and joined the group. Some didn't seem to know the steps, but they joined in, clapping and moving to the rhythm. The contagious beat pushed the drowsiness from Angel's head. For a second, she found herself nodding along.

"Angel?!"

Someone touched her shoulder. Angel whirled around and nearly froze in shock. Justice Waters stood before her in her baggy East Park Steppers T-shirt and black gym shorts. Angel felt a storm of confusion and embarrassment whirl inside her, and she instinctively recoiled and backed away. Had Justice heard about what happened? Was she about to insult her or be disgusted?

"You like steppin'?" Justice asked.

Angel blinked. The question took her by surprise. She could barely speak.

"Um . . . I . . . I don't know," she stammered.

"We practice Mondays at 3:15. I'm still learning, but this is a good group. We're not part of any of the drama at school, you know? Plus, it's free unless you want a T-shirt," she said, pointing to hers. "Try it out and see if you like it. You're not the only beginner."

Angel studied Justice. Wasn't she going to say anything about the text LaDonna sent in history class? Did she really think what Sharice told everyone was a joke? What was she thinking?

"No thanks."

"Come on," Justice said and grabbed Angel's arm. "Try it!"

"I can't. Plus, my backpack and stuff." Angel pointed to her backpack and shook her head.

"That's okay," Justice shouted over the increasing noise of the steppers. "Everyone leaves their stuff in Robin's car right over here. Robin's like our coach. She's a senior at Lincoln. It's okay." Justice pointed to the tall young woman who looked almost as if she could be Justice's older sister. Robin was facing the group and calling instructions.

"But I can't," Angel protested. "I've never done it."

"Neither has anybody until they try it the first time," Justice said with a laugh. "It's fun. You'll see. Come on!"

Justice dragged Angel to Robin's car to drop off her belongings and then led her back into the group of steppers. Angel was relieved that Justice chose to stay in the back where nobody could

84

really see them.

"Listen to Robin," Justice shouted. "She calls out what to do, while she's doing it the first time. Then we do the same steps again with her, okay?"

Angel nodded and listened as Robin called out the steps.

"Left, left, right, kick, clap, slap, turn!"

The group shouted back while copying her moves.

At first, Angel felt clumsy and slow. She fought the urge to return to her bench. But with each movement, she realized no one seemed to notice or care if she missed a step. As she relaxed, the steps gradually became easier.

"Right, right, clap, clap, slap, left, kick!"

Each time Robin called out, Angel concentrated on her own feet and repeated the steps quietly to herself again and again. Soon she was totally into the rhythm. When she finally looked up, Justice was grinning and shaking her head.

"Girl, you said you never stepped before. I *know* that can't be true. You're a natural. You haven't missed a beat!" she said during a quick break.

"Really, it's my first time," Angel

said with a laugh. "It helps to chant out the steps while you're doing them. Kind of like a poem or song."

"You definitely are better than me when I started! The first time I saw everyone here, I was like, 'There is no way I'm doin' this, 'cause it's usually like I've got two left feet,'" she said with a laugh. "Oh, here we go!"

Robin started calling out steps again, and the two girls chanted, kicked, stomped, and slapped along. Angel found herself grinning as she moved in rhythm with the group. At one point, Angel felt as if her feet were off the ground, as if she were flying, lifted by the drum-like noise that held them all in sync. She couldn't believe how such a terrible day had turned around. Following Robin's lead, Angel lost track of time until she heard the ringing of church bells above all the shouting and clapping. Alarmed, she glanced at someone's watch and saw it was 4:30.

"Oh no!" Angel said, turning to Justice. "I didn't realize how late it was. I need to pick up my little sister from the babysitter."

"That's cool," Justice said as she wiped her forehead. "We're done anyway.

Which way are you going?"

"Over to 35th," Angel said, rushing to get her things from Robin's car.

"I can go part way with you," Justice said as she draped her braids over her shoulder and grabbed her bags. "We live right over—oh no."

"What?" Angel followed Justice's gaze to a blue sports car. It was the same car she had seen on Friday. Some older kids were sitting on the hood. Another was in the driver's seat. Leaning against the passenger door, with an ugly sneer on her face, was LaDonna Burns.

Chapter 8

"Just who I was lookin' for," LaDonna barked, eyeing Justice.

"Ignore them," Justice said, looking tense but speaking quietly to Angel as she adjusted her backpack. "LaDonna's ignorant."

"It's just like I told you in school. You know it's true now, right?" LaDonna beamed as if she just won an argument. "Looks like she's tryin' to hook up with you, too! Y'all look so cute doing that little dance together." The two boys on the hood snickered. The girl sitting next to them mumbled something and pointed at Angel. All of them laughed.

Angel tried to inhale, but she felt as if the air had been punched out of her. Shame rushed to her face, but another feeling came bubbling up with it: anger.

Hot and searing, it spread through her like flames.

What was LaDonna's problem anyway? Why couldn't she just mind her own business? Did she really think it was okay to treat other people this way?

"Are y'all deaf?" LaDonna yelled.

Angel tried to avoid looking at her, but out of the corner of her eye, she saw LaDonna step from the car toward them. She stopped on the sidewalk directly in their path, blocking their way.

"Don't act like you can't hear me!" LaDonna huffed. She turned to her friends as she spoke. The girl behind LaDonna glanced nervously around the park. The boys on the car shrugged and looked at each other uncomfortably. For a second, no one spoke.

Finally Justice gave an exaggerated sigh, locking eyes with LaDonna. "We can hear you. We're just not *listening* to you. There's a difference, in case you couldn't figure it out."

One of the boys sitting on the car snickered.

"Oh, man. Girl fight!" said the other one.

LaDonna stepped forward so she was inches from Justice, raising her finger and pointing it like a gun.

"You best not be startin' with me, Miss Ugly Braids. I'll ruin you just like I did your girlfriend, *Gayngel*. And then you gonna be sorry you ever messed with me," LaDonna threatened.

Angel backed away from LaDonna, but Justice didn't flinch. Instead she made an exaggerated sad face and said, "Oh, no! I'm sooo upset LaDonna Burns doesn't like me. What on earth will I do?"

One of the boys laughed out loud. For an instant, LaDonna seemed confused.

"Anyway, you can say what you want," Justice continued, rolling her eyes as if she were suddenly bored. "No one really cares about your opinion. I know I don't."

"Oh, snap!" the same boy said.

LaDonna's eyes widened. She popped her gum angrily.

"That shows what you know, Justice Waters. It ain't my *opinion* about Angel, it's facts." LaDonna spoke in a rush as if she was desperate to get out the words. Angel noticed a red smear of lipstick on her teeth as she went on.

"Sharice told me how Angel don't like boys and how she was stupid enough to write it in some notebook and that she

90

was gonna ask *you* to go to the party
. . . I mean in *that* way. It's the truth!
Sharice and I been tellin' and textin'
everybody, so now everybody knows—"

"Whatever." Justice cut LaDonna off
with a dismissive wave of her hand. "No
one cares. Seriously, LaDonna. What
century do you even live in? Come on,
Angel."

Justice stepped around LaDonna,
who glared angrily, her hands on her
hips, a look of desperation in her eyes.

"Whatsa matter, *Gayngel?* Too scared
to say anything? Gotta let your *girlfriend*
protect you?"

Angel kept walking, but LaDonna
ran alongside her, yelling in her ear.

"Well, you can forget about thinking
you're all that! Sharice told me the only
reason Trey asked you to the party was
because of that phony text. He never
wanted to go with you! Me and Sharice
are tight now. She told me that she can
hook me up with Trey easy, and she's
gonna do it," LaDonna barked. "Whatcha
gonna do about *that?*"

Angel froze. An unusual calm swept
over her. She turned slowly until she
was eye-to-eye with LaDonna. She could
see cruel satisfaction on LaDonna's face,

as if she sensed victory.

"It's great if Trey wants to go to the party with you, LaDonna. But I don't believe it. I don't think he'd want to go anywhere with you," Angel said steadily. "He seems too nice. And you seem too rude and mean for him. Plus, you got lipstick on your teeth."

Justice snorted and put her hands to her face. "Whoa!" she exclaimed.

LaDonna's jaw dropped as if she had just been slapped.

Angel turned away quickly and joined Justice. Together they headed out of East Park.

Justice began giggling as soon as they left the park. By the time they reached the corner, she broke into loud raucous laughter and had to lean against a fence until she could catch her breath. Angel smiled but kept glancing back at the park. What if LaDonna came after them?

"Oh, man, Angel," Justice finally said, wiping her eyes. "I would never have expected you to say something like *that!* The look on LaDonna's face. That may be one of the funniest things I've ever seen!"

"I usually don't say things like that, but she just got to me," Angel admitted, unable to stop herself from grinning.

"That's 'cause she's a jerk and a rude loudmouth who had it coming to her. That girl's only happy if she's putting someone else down."

"Yeah," Angel agreed, looking back at the park one last time. "But why does she have to be like that?"

"Who knows. There's lots of reasons why people are bullies. Maybe her parents are mean to her. Maybe she's unhappy. Actually, sometimes I kinda feel sorry for her," Justice said.

"I don't, not after what she did to me today," Angel said, remembering the moment in history class. Angel felt a twinge of the old familiar awkwardness. At the park, she had so much fun, she had forgotten about her terrible day. But now, she recalled it all like a nightmare. Only it was true. What did Justice think? Did she believe what LaDonna said? And what about LaDonna's texts? The questions rolled through Angel's mind in waves.

Justice nodded. "Whatever her reasons, it's wrong for her to think it's an insult or funny to announce that someone is gay," Justice said. "It's not like it's 1950."

93

Angel almost tripped at Justice's words. "What?" she asked, struggling to hide her surprise. She hadn't expected Justice to come right out and talk about what was on her mind. Didn't she feel weird or embarrassed?

"You know," Justice said, giving Angel a funny look. "Her whole big deal about finding out something about you and acting like it's something you should be afraid or ashamed of. Who cares? No one."

Angel's mouth suddenly went dry. Her heart jumped in her chest as if it had just broken out of a cage. She could barely speak or turn her head to meet Justice's gaze.

"So, you mean," Angel said in a small voice, "that you . . . you don't care if I . . . I mean if someone is, or thinks they might be . . . you know?" Her last words came out in a whisper.

"Gay? Of course I don't care! My Uncle Kyle is gay. He and Uncle Raymond got married two years ago. They spend Christmas at our house every year with their daughter, my little cousin Sophia. They're the best uncles and fathers ever, and—"

"Wait," Angel blurted, struggling to

make sense of what she was hearing. "They're married and have a daughter? Are you serious? Everyone's okay with that?"

Justice laughed and shook her head, her braids dancing around. "Girl, where you been? Of course everyone's okay with it. Things have changed. It's not like it used to be."

"Not for everyone," Angel huffed. "Look at LaDonna and Sharice."

Justice nodded and frowned. "Yeah, there's always gonna be the haters, you know? It's like what Ms. Warner was talking about on Friday."

"Ms. Warner?" Angel asked, confused. "She said something about gay people?"

"No, not exactly," Justice said as the girls stopped at a crosswalk. "She was talking about how during Civil Rights some white people couldn't stand to see black and white people together. Remember?"

Angel nodded, recalling the story of Emmett Till. "But that was different."

"Yes and no," Justice replied. "It's all people hatin' on other people just because they're different. Getting angry and hurtful about who someone loves is just wrong. It just *is*. See what I mean?"

95

Angel nodded, feeling an odd mix of relief and embarrassment. She couldn't believe she and Justice were actually talking about gay people. And yet she couldn't help wondering: What did Justice think about her? Did she believe what Sharice and LaDonna said? Did it bother her?

"So, I gotta take a left up East Street here," Justice said, interrupting Angel's thoughts. "You still headed down 35th?"

"Yeah, I live off Greene Street. Going through East Park isn't the way I usually go home," Angel explained. "But I'm glad I went that way today," she added, suddenly feeling self-conscious.

"Me too!" Justice said brightly. "Girl, you got it goin' on with the steppin'. We can go every Monday, and then starting in summer, they meet up three times a week. You'll be taking Robin's place and leading everyone before long."

"I don't know about that," Angel said with a laugh. "Count me in for Monday, though." She could hardly believe Justice was being so friendly.

Are we friends now? Angel wondered. *Is this how it's going to be from now on?* She hoped so.

"See you tomorrow, then. And Angel

. . ." Justice leaned over and gave her a friendly hug. "Don't let the haters get you down. Most people aren't like La-Donna or Sharice. Most people are gonna be happy that you're just being yourself. Remember that."

Angel thanked Justice and watched her disappear into the crowd on East Street. Then she headed home, her head a swirl of worry, joy, and gratitude.

She knew she was later than usual, but it was still early enough that Dionne would be down the hall at Ms. Alexander's apartment. Mom wouldn't be home for two hours and would never even know she was late. Maybe, if Mom was having a good day, Angel would even tell her she had tried out stepping at East Park with a new friend.

A new friend! The words made her smile.

Angel was rushing down the hall to the babysitter's when she heard a door open behind her. She turned to see Mom burst into the hall, a mix of fury and relief in her eyes.

"Angel McAllister, where have you *been?!*" she shouted.

"Mom . . . you're home?"

"Yeah, I've been here for hours

worrying about you." Mom stepped closer to Angel, studying her face. "Are you okay? Where were you?"

"I was in school," Angel answered quickly, hoping her voice sounded natural.

"Why are you lying to me?"

"What?"

"Mr. Collins called me at work today. He thought you went home sick. He was checking on you," Mom explained. Angel felt as if the floor had suddenly given way beneath her feet. "That's when I spoke to your principal. He said you missed all your afternoon classes. No one at school had any idea where you were."

Angel stared at her shoes, unable to look into her mother's piercing gaze.

"So I'm gonna ask you again. What's going on, Angel?" Mom asked. "Where were you?"

Angel sighed, unsure where to begin or how to answer.

"It's complicated," she said finally.

"Come inside right now," Mom said, pulling her by the arm into the apartment. "I want to hear everything. And I want to hear the truth."

Chapter 9

"It's really not a big deal," Angel insisted for the third time. She folded her arms and looked away, trying to hide the emotions swirling in her chest. How could she explain what Sharice and LaDonna had done without telling Mom the full truth? How could she risk letting Mom know what she was? There was no way.

"Cutting school?" Mom snapped. "Disappearing for half the day? Lying to your teacher about being sick? This is a very big deal, Angel!"

Angel felt tears welling in her eyes. She fought to conceal them, to push them back, but she couldn't help it. One threatened to slip down her face. Angel wiped it away quickly, but Mom noticed. For the first time in weeks, she seemed totally focused.

"What is it, Angel?" she pleaded. "Tell me what's wrong! What happened?"

"I've had some trouble at school . . ."

Just then, Dionne came down the hall into the living room. "What's wrong? Why's everyone yelling?" she asked as she walked over to Angel.

"Dionne, remember how I told you Angel and I were gonna have a grown-up talk when she came home? We're having that talk right now, baby. I need you to go play in your room until we're done, okay?" Mom gently squeezed Dionne's shoulder and led her back to her room. Angel knew Dionne would sit by her door and listen, like always. Angel crossed her arms and prepared for the questions Mom was about to ask. She braced herself as her mother took a deep breath and approached her.

"What kinda trouble?"

Angel paused, searching for words to satisfy Mom but still keep her secret hidden. "It's just that there are some kids that . . . that give me a hard time sometimes," she said finally.

"Like bullies?" Mom asked, her forehead wrinkling with concern.

"Yeah, I guess so."

"Who, Angel?"

"It doesn't matter."

"It does to me!" Mom insisted. "Why would anyone bother you, of all people? There's nothing about you that—"

"It's because I'm different, Mom!" Angel blurted, surprised at how loud her voice became. "I'm *not* like everyone else! And sometimes when you're . . . different, people give you a hard time."

Mom looked at Angel with a puzzled expression. *"Different?* You're a regular fourteen-year-old girl. What are these kids saying to you?"

Angel could feel Dionne listening behind the door. There was no way she could have an honest conversation about this with Mom. Not now. Maybe not ever.

"It's just stupid stuff," Angel said, wishing Mom would stop asking for details. "I told you it's not a big deal. Can we just forget it?"

"If it's not a big deal, why'd you sneak out of school in the middle of the day?"

Angel shrugged. She remembered the moment in the hall with Omar and Trevor. "I got upset, that's all. I'm over it now. Look, can we drop this, Mom? I've got a poetry assignment to finish and a test to study for."

Mom shook her head and grabbed her phone.

"Who are you calling?"

"The school," Mom said. "We're gonna get to the bottom of this right now—"

"No!" Angel yelled. "You'll only make it worse."

"Worse? You're so scared you won't even talk to me. I'm not sure what's going on over there, but I am sure your principal needs to know about it."

"Mom, please!" Angel grabbed her mother's hands before she placed the call. "The year's almost over. Just let it go. *Please*," Angel begged.

"But you'll see the same kids next year in high school. We need to fix this."

Angel's jaw clenched. In a flash, anger and resentment joined the storm of feelings raging in her chest. Maybe on a different day, Mom's concern would be comforting. But after the past few weeks, it was like an insult. A slap in the face.

"*Fix it?* You can't fix anything right now," Angel yelled, feeling her eyes beginning to burn.

"What are you saying?"

"You talk about *me* disappearing? What about *you*, Mom?! Where have *you* been? You might be here sitting on the couch, but you're not here with us."

Mom winced as if she had been hit. Angel knew it was wrong to speak to her mother this way, but she couldn't stop. It was as if a dam had burst and a flood came pouring out.

"You act as if you're the only one around here upset about Dad. Like it's okay for you to shut down and let things go. But that's not fair, Mom. And then you say you can fix it. Have you even looked around? I mean, the house is a mess. There's never any food around, Dionne is lonely, and you don't seem to notice! It's like you don't even care about us anymore," Angel fumed.

"I know it hasn't been easy these past weeks, but I'm doing what I can. Okay?"

"Well that's not enough, Mom," Angel grumbled, turning away so she didn't have to see her mother's glistening eyes. Mom tried to hug her, and as much as she missed her mother's embrace, Angel felt as if it wasn't meant for her. That if Mom knew the truth, she might never want to hug her again. The knowledge was like an invisible wall that Mom's touch couldn't pierce.

"Is that what this is all about?"

Mom asked finally. "Dad and me?"

Angel took a deep breath. The wall between them seemed to thicken. Angel didn't want to lie, but she couldn't say the words anchored to the tip of her tongue. *"I think I'm gay, Mom."*

Instead she nodded, feeling her mother's arms on her shoulders. Her touch almost burned.

"So where did you go?" Mom asked rubbing her back. "I mean, when you left school."

"East Park," Angel admitted. "I went to sit on the bench where Dad and I used to sit."

Dionne emerged at the doorway to her room. "You went to East Park without me?" she moaned. "Why? I wanted to go, too."

Mom's eyes widened at the mention of the park. It was as if she had just remembered something important, something she had forgotten long ago.

"You told me you'd take me, Angel," Dionne said as she came into the living room holding her crumpled elephant. "Remember the day before Momma got really mad and broke the dishes?"

Mom took a deep breath as if she had just surfaced out of water. She gazed at

Dionne's sad face and then at Angel. Then she glanced around the apartment, first toward the overflowing ashtrays, then at the dusty table, the laundry piled on the floor, the dirty dishes in the sink, the empty wine bottle next to the sofa. Tears welled in her eyes and her shoulders slumped. Angel had never seen her mother look so defeated.

Watching her, Angel felt guilty about her outburst. "I'm sorry, Mom," she said, unsure how to comfort her.

"Me too, Momma," Dionne added, giving her a hug and then handing her the old elephant, as if it could help her feel better. Mom smiled and cried at the same time.

"No, don't you two apologize to me. You didn't do anything wrong. I couldn't ask for better girls. You just reminded me of that," she said, wiping her eyes. "All this is *me*. I created it. I need to deal with it." Mom looked around the messy apartment as if she were seeing it for the first time. A hush spread over them for a few moments.

Dionne finally broke the silence.

"Why don't we all go to East Park?" she asked. "You too, Momma. It'll make us all feel better. It always does. We can get ice cream, too."

"Now?" said Angel.

Mom gave a teary smile.

"I can't, baby. I've got a few things I need to do around here right now. Why don't you two go, if Angel's okay with it? Be home by 6:30. Next time, I'll come along," she said, looking soberly at the apartment. "I promise."

"Can we go, Angel? Can we go?" Dionne begged.

Angel smiled at her little sister and gave her a hug. "Let's do it."

Dionne cheered.

"I got a dance I want to teach you, too, once we get there," Angel added.

Mom stopped Angel at the door before she left. "I don't know why anyone would ever pick on you," she said, her eyes still glistening. "If they had any sense, they'd see there ain't a better big sister or daughter in the world. Y'hear me? Thank you for taking care of us these past few weeks."

Mom hugged her then. Angel returned the embrace, but she still felt the pang inside, as if something were missing, the hug incomplete. *Will it always be this way from now on?* Angel wondered. There was a part of her that Mom didn't know about, and it ached, unloved, as she closed the door.

From the hallway, Angel heard the muffled roar of their old vacuum cleaner coming to life.

Angel could barely believe the transformation when they returned from the park. In less than two hours, Mom had cleaned up everything.

The living room furniture glimmered. Gospel music drifted from the radio in the kitchen. All the front windows were open, allowing the late-spring breeze to circulate through the once musty rooms. The piles of laundry were gone, and the washing machine whirred and churned in the background.

"Wow!" Dionne said in amazement as she looked around.

Angel noticed the table was set for dinner. Mom emerged from the kitchen carrying a large pot of steaming spaghetti and sauce. Fresh rolls were piled on a cookie sheet next to where Angel usually sat. Butter was on the table, too.

"You made dinner?!" Dionne exclaimed. "It's like the old days, Angel!"

"I didn't have time to get much," Mom said. "But I'll do a bigger grocery trip tomorrow."

"Mom, this looks great," Angel said, realizing she was hungry. In all the excitement of the day, she had barely eaten.

"Girls, I want to apologize for how I've been acting these past few weeks," Mom said as she passed the food around the table.

"You mean because you've been so grouchy and sleepy?" Dionne asked bluntly. "And upset all the time?"

Angel would have laughed if the topic weren't so serious and her mother didn't seem so nervous.

"That's right, baby," Mom agreed, patting Dionne's hand and explaining how sad she had been about the split-up with Dad. "He is moving in with his new girlfriend just a block away, and I . . . I can't be near that. It's not good for me or for you girls, either."

"What are you saying, Mom?" asked Angel.

"For a while I've been thinking about moving to the other side of the city. Your Dad just pushed up the timeline. I know a neighborhood where we'd be closer to the beach and my job. It's got good schools, too. Bluford High for you, Angel. You could get a brand-new start away from those kids. Plus they got a nice afterschool program for you, Dionne, at a place called Little Learning Spot. There's even a supermarket nearby—"

"You mean we're moving?" Dionne interrupted.

"Not too far away," Mom assured her. "You could still visit Dad or East Park, but I think a change would do us good."

"Could we go to the beach on weekends?" Dionne asked hopefully. "And maybe ride that merry-go-round I went on last year?"

"Sure," Mom said with a grin. "It would take some adjusting, but I think the three of us might like it. What do you think, Angel?"

A brand new start. The words bounced through Angel's mind like lines from a poem. It was an answer, a way to escape from her ruined reputation, the stares, the comments, and the snickers. A way to regain her privacy and avoid being another "Jeremy" at Lincoln High.

Sure, she would lose Sharice for good, but that friendship was already ruined. Then there was Justice, the one person who made her actually want to stay at Lincoln. But that connection wouldn't have to end, Angel figured. She wouldn't let it. They wouldn't be that far away.

"Angel?" Mom asked.

Next year beckoned like a blank page in her mind, an entry not yet written, a place where she could try whatever she wanted without anyone laughing at her.

Step dancing. Maybe even cheer-leading. Or something else?

Her thoughts soared with possibilities.

"It sounds great, Mom," she said. And she meant it.

Later that night, Angel sat hunched over her notebook revising her poetry assignment for Mr. Collins's class when her phone rang. She didn't recognize the number.

"Hello?"

"Hey Angel. It's Win. Sorry to bother you. I just, well, I didn't see you in school after everything . . . and I wanted to make sure you're okay."

"I'm fine," Angel said hesitantly, curious to know what he had heard.

"I'm sorry about what happened." Win stammered as he spoke. She could picture him running his hand nervously through his hair. "I didn't want you to think I was mad or anything."

She didn't know how to respond. Did

he believe what was going on? She wanted to know but was afraid to ask. There was a long pause. "Thanks," she finally said.

"Look, Angel. I know what LaDonna and Sharice are saying, and I just wanted to tell you that none of that matters to me, okay? I . . . I hope we can still be friends."

Angel sighed with surprise and relief. "Of course, Win! I'm so glad you still want to be friends with me, especially after all that drama."

"You mean after my excellent display of fighting skills?" he joked. "Seriously, if you still want to go to the party, we can go together, as friends. But it's cool if you don't want to."

"Well, I'd like to go with you, Win," Angel admitted. "But after everything, I don't think that's a good idea. Besides, I was supposed to go with Trey, Sharice, and Marcus. I doubt that's gonna happen now, but I think it's better for everybody if I just stay home."

"Well, I don't think Sharice and Marcus are even going anymore," Win said. "They were arguing after school today. It was bad. I doubt those two wanna be anywhere together."

"Really?"

"Yeah, I figured I'd let you know in case you were still making plans," Win explained.

They spoke for a few more minutes, and Angel fought an urge to call Sharice and find out what happened. But each time she looked at her journal, she could hear Sharice telling her secrets to La-Donna. The betrayal still stung like an open wound.

"Let me get back to you about the party. Is that okay?"

"Sure, Angel," Win said, sounding both relieved and disappointed.

"And no matter what, Win, thanks," Angel said shyly. "Thanks for being my friend."

Chapter 10

Angel felt knots in her stomach as she left her apartment the next morning. It was the last day of middle school. The final time she would have to face everyone again. The last day with LaDonna. It almost didn't seem real.

Out of habit, Angel looked for Sharice on the corner of Greene Street. A twinge of sadness stabbed at her as she gazed down Sharice's block, remembering the countless times they had walked together. Part of her still couldn't believe what happened.

"I would never have done that to you, Sharice," Angel mumbled, passing by the lonely corner.

"Hey, Angel!" came a familiar voice from the other side of the street. "Hurry up!"

Angel looked up to see Justice. She had come to meet her!

"C'mon. You can't be late on our last day," she said, with a flip of her braids. "Can you believe it? We're done after this!"

"No, I can't," Angel replied, grateful to not have to walk alone on the final day of school. "It doesn't seem real that we're done with middle school."

"I know, right?! But really all we're doin' is movin' down the street," Justice said, glancing toward Lincoln High. "I wonder if we'll be in the same classes next year."

"I doubt it," Angel confessed. "It looks like my family is moving this summer. If we do, I'm going to Bluford."

"For real?" Justice's smile suddenly twisted into a frown. "Why?"

"My parents just split up. My dad and his new girlfriend are moving to our neighborhood. My mom can't handle that. She needs a fresh start somewhere else." Angel paused. "I can't blame her. To be honest, I kinda feel the same way."

"I'm sorry about your parents, girl." Justice shook her head somberly as they paused at a traffic light. "That's just wrong for like a hundred different reasons."

"It is," Angel agreed. "But I keep

114

telling myself it might be good to start fresh, you know? Get away from all this. No one knows me there. Maybe at Bluford things will be different. Maybe I'll even try something new like . . ." Angel glanced at Justice and wondered if she would laugh at her. "Like cheerleading, even."

"You totally should!" Justice said. "You're a natural at stepping. After stepping, cheering should be easy. Bluford'll get a whole new Angel," she said with a grin.

"That's gotta be better than the old one, right?"

Justice's grin faded.

"That's not what I meant, Angel. What I'm saying is you don't need to *hide* the real you. Don't be ashamed of who you are. My grandma told me that every day when kids teased me about my hair or my skin. For some, I was too light. For others, I was too dark. Whatever. This is what I am. This is how God made me," she said, pointing to her face. "The new Angel is who you are. Just be you."

Angel nodded. She knew Justice was right, but even so she wished she could be her "real" self when she was ready— not when some bully announced it to the whole school. She wouldn't let that happen at Bluford, where there might be other LaDonnas. Or worse.

"Yeah, well, I'm not sure everyone's ready for the new Angel," she said, eyeing a group of students walking to school ahead of them. Lincoln High loomed to their right like a fortress.

"That's their problem, not yours," Justice said. "Anyway, when you make the cheerleading team, I'm comin' to watch you cheer."

"For real?" Angel asked, touched by her words. "You'd do that?"

"Why not? We're friends, right?"

Angel couldn't help but smile. "Yeah, but I gotta make the team first."

"Please, Angel. I'll make sure you're ready. We *got* this."

"I don't know. It's not always about how you move," Angel replied. She struggled to picture herself as a cheerleader. "Girls like me . . . don't really get to be cheerleaders."

"Girls like you? What's that supposed to mean?"

"You know . . . ," Angel said, meeting Justice's gaze. "Besides, I'm not popular or pretty. I'm not like Sharice or LaDonna—"

"At least you don't wear lipstick on

your teeth," Justice snorted.

"I'm serious," Angel replied. "You know there's gonna be another LaDonna at Bluford."

"So?" Justice snapped as they made the final turn toward the middle school. "If there is, she doesn't get to decide what you can or can't do. Back in the day, it was that way, but not anymore. Girls like you or me or whoever, we have a chance. That's why you gotta at least try. And if you don't, I'm gonna get mad at you, Angel McAllister," she added, her eyes somehow playful and serious at the same time.

"Well, then, I guess I'm tryin' out for cheerleading next year," Angel said.

"Good. You better!" Justice replied as they entered Lincoln Middle and headed in opposite directions. "See you in history."

The main corridor was louder and felt more packed than ever. The final day seemed to give everyone an extra jolt of excitement. Lockers crashed and thudded as students shouted to each other on the way to class.

Angel darted through the crowded hallway, hoping to slip by unnoticed. With each step, she braced herself for stares, whispers, and jokes, but no one approached her.

"Just one day," she repeated to herself as she ducked her head down and moved toward her locker. That's when she saw Omar smirking at her from across the hall.

"There she is!" Omar said with an ugly sneer. "Miss me?" He made wet kissing noises, but then stopped suddenly.

"You got a problem?" A deep voice growled from behind her. She turned around to see Marcus weaving toward her.

Omar hesitated and appeared confused. Several kids stopped to see what was happening. "Just jokin' around, bro." He shrugged. "Ain't no big thing."

"Yeah, well your joke ain't funny," Marcus snapped, glaring at Omar.

"Sorry."

"You better be. Next time you got something to say to her, you say it to me," Marcus growled. "You hear me?"

Omar nodded. A teacher approached from the end of the hallway and students dispersed.

"Thanks, Marcus," Angel said, almost too surprised to speak. "You didn't have to do that."

"Yes, I did," Marcus grumbled. "I heard

118

all about what's goin' on, and it ain't right. I can't believe Sharice would think I'd be down with what she and LaDonna did to you. She got me all wrong. I'm done with her. Done."

Angel remembered what Win had said about Marcus and Sharice fighting. She felt a twinge of guilt about them breaking up. Wherever she was, Sharice would be devastated. Angel was sure of it.

"Sorry about you and Sharice," she said, surprised he was so angry about what Sharice had done.

"I'm not!" Marcus said with a laugh. "It's all good. I mean, I shoulda known after that crazy text she sent Trey. I shoulda started running in the other direction right then."

Overhead, the first period warning bell rang out.

"Anyway, I'll see you later, Angel," he said, heading off to class. "Let me know if anyone else messes with you. They'll have to deal with *me*," he added as he disappeared down the hall.

Angel felt stunned as she made her way to class. Her classmates had heard the rumors, and yet their reactions were unlike anything she had expected.

They know, she marveled to herself

as she entered the classroom, *and some of them don't care.* She could hardly believe it. *They know, and it's okay.*

Justice sat next to Angel in history class, instead of her usual spot across the room. LaDonna avoided them completely. Instead, she sat with her arms crossed, glaring out the window as if her neck were somehow locked in that position.

As Ms. Warner handed out their graded exams, Win leaned over and whispered.

"Angel, I'm going to the party with Jazelle Thompson. *She* actually asked *me!* Can you believe it?"

"That *is* hard to believe," Justice answered with a playful grin.

"I know!" Win agreed, his eyes widening as he spoke. "She even said I was brave when I stood up for you."

"She's right, Win," Angel replied. "She's lucky she gets to go with you. I mean that."

Win blushed and shrugged awkwardly just as Ms. Warner began class.

Later, in English, Angel noticed Sharice had chosen a seat on the opposite side of the room, as far away from her as possible. Not once did she even look at

Angel during class, though Angel tried several times to get her attention. Sharice's eyes were pink and puffy, and she kept blowing her nose.

In all their time as friends, Angel had rarely seen Sharice cry. She wanted to talk to her but then remembered how disgusted Sharice had been when she stormed out of her room.

"I'm sorry, Sharice," she thought to herself as she reread her poetry assignment one last time.

Trey entered the classroom just before the bell, eyeing her nervously.

"Can we talk after school today?" he asked. She could tell others in the class were listening. She could see Trey noticed it, too.

"Okay," she agreed, wondering if he felt the same way as his brother. She noticed he avoided looking at Sharice, who sat stone-faced except for a quick sniffle when he took his seat.

"So this is it, everyone," Mr. Collins announced. "Your last chance to make a contribution to poetry in middle school."

There was a scattering of groans and sighs.

"Come on, now," Mr. Collins said, glancing in the direction of the loudest protests. "This is your very last English assignment at Lincoln Middle. Think of this poem as your last golden moment, your swan song, your farewell, your final hurrah!"

A few students chuckled. Angel felt a nervous twinge in her stomach. She had finished the assignment days ago but decided to rewrite it last night. The talk with Mom, step dancing at East Park with Justice, the idea of a new start—she wanted all of it reflected in her poem.

When Mr. Collins finally called Angel up to read, she glanced once at Sharice, who she knew was listening, and then at Trey, who watched her intently. The poem was her answer to what Mr. Collins had asked her once in class: "Why does the caged bird sing?" She had discovered an answer, one that came to her lips like a song:

"Why would a bird locked in a cage
Ever want to sing a song?
All the free birds sing together
Because they feel like they belong.

"But the bird who's not allowed to fly
Into this new spring day

Sits inside her cage by herself
And sings out loud anyway.

"It may seem strange to hear her song
It may be hard for some to see
How a bird that's not like all the rest
Can sing just like she's free.

"The song rings out as clear as sky
Loud and strong and free
'Cause you can't lock away her heart
You can never cage her dreams!"

*   *   *

At lunch, Angel mistakenly headed toward her old table with Sharice when she heard voices call out to her.

"Angel! Over here!" She was surprised to see Justice waving at her. Marcus sat across from her.

"Looks like we both had to find a different table, huh, Angel?" Marcus said as he nodded across the cafeteria at Sharice, who sat alone, hunched over her phone with a scowl on her face. Two tables over, LaDonna snapped her gum and chattered away with her same old circle of friends. "I wish we did this sooner."

"Me too," Justice said.

"Why isn't Sharice with LaDonna?" Angel asked.

"Are you really surprised?" Justice asked as she speared a chicken nugget. "Once she found out Sharice wasn't her ticket to hooking up with Trey, she dropped her."

"Wow. That's kinda sad."

"You know what's really sad?" Marcus asked with a fake sad face. "Me not having anyone to go to the party with now. *That's* a tragedy."

"Oh, boo hoo," Justice said, and she tossed a carrot stick at him playfully. "Are you really that upset about missing the party?"

"Actually, it's supposed to be pretty cool," Marcus replied with a grin. "I mean, a live DJ and free all-you-can-eat pizza. That's all I need." Suddenly, he turned to Angel. "You still going with Trey?"

Angel shrugged. "I don't know. He disappeared after English class. I doubt he wants to go—at least, not with me."

"You're wrong about that, Angel," Marcus said, suddenly looking serious. "He told me he'd really like to go with you, especially now. You know . . . as friends."

"Really?" Angel noticed he seemed to

pause on the last word as if it had special meaning.

"Hey, I know!" Justice said, snapping her fingers excitedly. "Why don't all four of us go together—as friends! My granddad drives for a limo service, and I know he'll hook us up with a ride!"

"Oh, man—a limo! You *know* I'm in," Marcus said, slapping his hand on the table. Then he looked at Justice shyly. "And it would be great to go with you, too, of course. I mean, with all of us. You in, Angel?"

Angel could hardly believe what they were asking. She was going to the party with Justice after all.

"Yeah," she cheered. "Let's do it!"

Marcus stood watch at Angel's locker at the end of the day, protecting her like a bodyguard until she had emptied her belongings and slammed shut the metal door for the last time.

Although the halls roared with students cheering and hollering, no one laughed or teased Angel as they made their final exit from Lincoln Middle School.

Outside, Trey and Justice waited. Trey approached Angel as soon as he saw her.

Justice and Marcus hung back to give them space.

"Angel, I just wanted to say, I'm sorry about all this party drama," he said nervously. "But if you still want to go, I'd really like to go with you as friends."

"I'm sorry too, but I think we should go. Justice is getting us a limo," Angel replied. "I still can't believe Sharice tricked both of us into going."

"Me neither. But it kind of makes sense though," he said with a knowing grin.

"What do you mean?"

"Let's just say. We have a lot in common. I know how tough it is, too," he said, his eyes locked on hers. "You understand?"

Angel's jaw dropped as his words sank in.

Trey was gay, too.

That's why he never went out with girls. That's why Marcus had gotten so furious at Sharice and why he was so protective of his brother's privacy. It all made sense.

Staring at Trey, Angel realized that she had never been as alone as she thought. There were others all around her, trapped in their own invisible cages.

Girls like me, she thought. *People like me.*

She glanced back at the middle school. It seemed smaller somehow, diminished by what she had learned.

"Now you understand?" Trey asked.

Angel nodded and smiled, blinking back tears of gratitude for her new friends and the secret she no longer carried alone.

The four of them left the middle school together, laughing about the party and the limo ride to come.

And for the first time, Angel's spirit soared, uncaged and unashamed.

Epilogue

On a warm summer day in early August, Angel stepped off the bus with Justice. They walked a few blocks, past a busy commercial strip with some restaurants she had never seen.

The Golden Grill. Niko's Pizza. Phat Burger.

They passed SuperFoods and then reached an enormous school sitting atop a shallow rise. Surrounded by a metal fence, the campus included a track, basketball courts, and a pristine football field framed by silver metal bleachers.

A large sign next to the field greeted them.

Welcome to Bluford High
Home of the Buccaneers

Angel's stomach tightened with nerves.

"There it is," Justice said. "Your new school. That paper says to drop off your cheerleading forms in the front office. Let's do it."

Angel looked at her friend and took a deep breath. A whole new world awaited her. She knew it would be different from middle school. New teachers. New kids. New enemies and, she hoped, new friends. Either way, Angel was ready.

She was grateful to put middle school behind her. She wouldn't reveal what happened there to anyone at her new school. The less her new classmates knew, the better. That was the way it had to be. The world would see a new Angel.

It was the fresh start she wanted. Angel seized it with both hands.

"Let's go," she said, walking to the front doors of Bluford High.

Stories to Experience
The Bluford Series

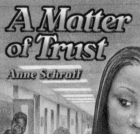

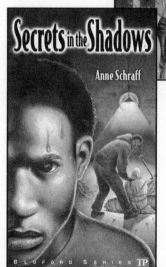

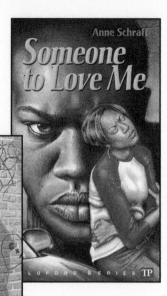

Anne Schraft

Someone to Love Me

BLUFORD SERIES TP

The Bully

Paul Langan

TP BLUFORD SER

The Gun

Paul Langan

BLUFORD SERIES TP

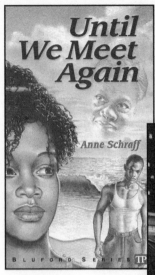

Until We Meet Again

Anne Schraff

BLUFORD SERIES

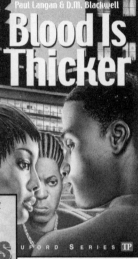

Paul Langan & D.M. Blackwell

Blood Is Thicker

BLUFORD SERIES

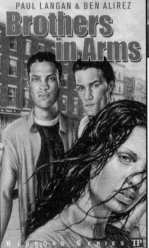

PAUL LANGAN & BEN ALIREZ

Brothers in Arms

BLUFORD SERIES

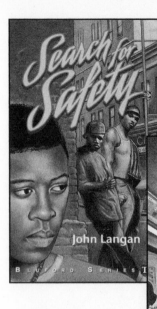

Search for Safety

John Langan

BLUFORD SERIES I

PEGGY KERN

No Way Out

BLUFORD SERIES TP

Paul Langan

Schooled

BLUFORD SERIES TP

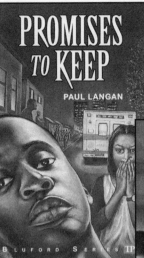

PROMISES TO KEEP

PAUL LANGAN

BLUFORD SERIES TP

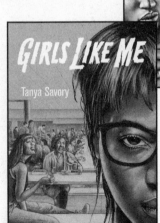

SURVIVOR

PAUL LANGAN

BLUFORD SERIES TP

GIRLS LIKE ME

Tanya Savory

BLUFORD SERIES TP

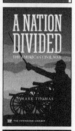

Modernized Classics

More TP Library Titles — Still only $2 per book!

Adventures of Tom Sawyer
Amazing Harry Houdini
Animal Rescue
Beasts of Tarzan
Black Beauty
Call of the Wild
Captains Courageous
Count of Monte Cristo
Great Expectations
Great Moments in Sports
Jane Eyre
John F. Kennedy
Jungle Book
King Arthur and His Knights
Last of the Mohicans
Little Women
Lost on the Mountain
The Mark of Zorro
Merry Adventures of Robin Hood
The Odyssey
Oliver Twist
Pollyanna
The Power of Love
Pride and Prejudice

The Prince and The Pauper
A Princess of Mars
Rebounding
Red Badge of Courage
Return of Tarzan
Robinson Crusoe
The Scarlet Letter
Scary Medical Stories
Scary Stories
The Sea-Wolf
Second Wind
Silas Marner
Swamp Curse
Swiss Family Robinson
A Tale of Two Cities
Tarzan of the Apes
Ten Real-Life Stories
Treasure Island
Uncle Tom's Cabin
Virginian
War of the Worlds
Warlord of Mars
White Fang
The Wizard of Oz

. . . and many, many more.

For more information and to order, visit
www.townsendpress.com